RōNIN: INSURRECTION

VOLUME 1

E. A. LILLEHOJ

I wish to thank Doug Howland, Matt Cook, Jack Ratliff and Helen Marlborough for reading and offering comments on earlier versions of this story. Thanks also to Joe Esposito for his patience and sense of humor.

North
Entsūji
Mount Hiei
Aki's home
Takano River
Otowa River
Enshōji
Kamo River
Market
Manshuin
First Street Temple District
Shirakawa Avenue
Ichijō residence
Konoe residence
Hachijō residence
Nijō residence
Silver Pavilion
Palace
Daimonji
Sento
Reikanji
Second Street
Kamo River
Second Street Castle
Third Street
Kyoto

CONTENTS

Aki: a young woman from northeastern Kyoto who delivers firewood it to aristocratic residences in Kyoto

Bunkai* (1629–?): Kūgon Bunkai; Sagami; daughter of Katatsuki Sōshin; served former Empress Tōfukumon'in at court before becoming a Zen nun and moving to Enshōji

Gohei: a middle-aged man; he meets Aki near the Silver Pavilion; formerly a porter in Edo

Gomi Toyonao* (1583–1660): the Second Street magistrate; Tanaka's boss's boss; second-in-command of the Office of the Kyoto Governor

Ishida Kurōbei: a young rōnin outlaw; aka Shining Blade

Natsu: mother of Aki; a woman from northeastern Kyoto who sells flowers grown in the Shirakawa area

Shimada Gorō: an older rōnin; former advisor to the father of Ishida Kurōbei

Tanaka Taisuke: deputy inspector in the Office of the Kyoto Governor; reporting to the commissioner, Wada Wakusei

SECONDARY CHARACTERS

Itakura Shigemune* (1586–1657): Kyoto governor; one of the top warrior lords serving the Tokugawa; responsible for the civil and judicial administration of Kyoto and eight neighboring regions

Mari: Granny Mari; elderly vendor of vegetables from a stall at Yamabana Market

Prince Hachijō Toshitada* (1619–62): relative of the Enshōji abbess; first cousin once removed of retired Emperor GoMizunoo

Sumi: maid in the kitchen of the Konoe mansion

The abbot of Manshuin* (1623–93): Reverend Ryōshō; tonsured prince; relative of the Enshōji abbess; younger brother of Prince Hachijō Toshitada; first cousin once removed of retired Emperor GoMizunoo

The Crab: agent working for Deputy Inspector Tanaka in the Office of the Kyoto Governor

The Mouse: kunoichi working for Deputy Inspector Tanaka in the Office of the Kyoto Governor

The Stork: kunoichi working for Deputy Inspector Tanaka in the Office of the Kyoto Governor

The Wolf: agent working for Deputy Inspector Tanaka in the Office of the Kyoto Governor

Wada Wakusei: commissioner in the Office of the Kyoto Governor; Tanaka's boss

OTHERS:

Daitsū Bunchi* (1619–97): founding abbess of Enshōji, a Zen convent at Shugakuin in northeastern Kyoto

Emperor GoMizunoo* (1596–1680): retired emperor (reigned 1611–29); father of the Enshōji abbess

Emperor GoKōmyō* (1633–54): current emperor (reigned 1643–54); son of retired Emperor GoMizunoo and half-brother of the Enshōji abbess

Katatsuki Sōshin* (?–1674): former imperial court lady; foster mother to the Enshōji abbess; founder of the sub-temple of Ryokuin'an at Enshōji

Prince Hachijō Toshihito* (1579–1629): imperial prince; younger brother of Emperor GoYōzei

Tokugawa shōguns: founders of the Edo warrior government; first shōgun = Tokugawa Ieyasu* (1542–1616; ruled 1603–05); second shōgun = Tokugawa Hidetada* (1579–1632, ruled 1605–23); third shōgun = Iemitsu* (1604–51; ruled 1623–51)

The lord of Kishū* (1602–71): Tokugawa Yorinobu; the tenth son of Tokugawa Ieyasu; named lord of Wakayama Domain

Yui Shōsetsu* (1605–51): deceased rōnin and martial arts instructor; owner of a shop selling armor; leader of the Edo Insurrection of 1651

PREFACE

At one time, Kyoto was praised as the capital of peace and tranquility. In the summer of 1654, however, Kyoto was anything but harmonious. Its streets were choked with thousands of discontented rōnin, or masterless warriors, determined to vent their pent-up frustrations. Reader, prepare to face a Kyoto rōnin revolt.

PART 1

BACKGROUND: RŌNIN AND THE TOKUGAWA PACIFICATION

You may already know, Educated Reader, that a leading general from the Tokugawa clan received the title of shōgun, just as decades-long civil wars were ending in Japan. Soon after, following a great battle victory in 1615, the Tokugawa shōgun cemented his grip on power, establishing a new capital in the east at Edo. Kyoto, the old capital, retained its venerated place, now with a governor appointed by the shōgun overseeing the city and enforcing laws flowing down from Edo. The massive edifice of Second Street Castle, Kyoto headquarters of the Tokugawa, announced for all to see that an Edo shōgun dominated the city.

In the early years of Tokugawa rule, shōguns concentrated on establishing peace, which is to say, they focused on imposing their will on all in the land. The shōgun claimed that his rule was a great blessing upon the realm, Kyoto included. As everyone realized, however, this blessing would result in the creation of a vast body of disgruntled and displaced rōnin.

Perhaps it was inevitable that in moments of Tokugawa vulnerability, the smoldering anger of rōnin exploded. One such moment followed the 1651 death of the third

Tokugawa shōgun, whose heir was merely a boy. A number of Edo rōnin had been waiting for this chance. Bursting through their restraints, they rose up to challenge the authority of the Edo Elders, a small group of regents advising the boy shōgun.

Before long, winds of dissatisfaction blew into the old capital, encouraging the Kyoto rōnin to launch their own revolt. Awaiting you, Intrepid Reader, is one such rōnin—Ishida Kurōbei, also known as Shining Blade.

"Spare change?" called out the monkey trainer. Sitting streetside in a market district in downtown Kyoto, the trainer held up a hemp cord in his withered hand. The cord was attached to the collar around the neck of a scrawny brown monkey, which was dressed in a child's jacket with a toy fan in one hand and a tiny black cap on its head.

As the monkey twirled, the trainer entreated onlookers, "A penny for my little friend?"

Pedestrians on Fourth Street had gathered to watch the performance. Some were taking a break from shopping. Others were idling away their morning. A woman in the crowd approached and tossed a coin into the trainer's begging bowl. The simian lifted its cap, bowed and resumed its spinning, eliciting applause from the crowd.

When the monkey stopped, the trainer picked up a stick to prod the creature. The monkey responded by hopping on one foot for a short while, but seeing the trainer set down his stick, the monkey came to a full stop. It reached back and scratched its hindquarters, prompting hoots of laughter from onlookers.

Hours earlier, shop owners on this block had unlocked their doors, raised their shutters and set out their goods. For sale here were pillows, pottery, incense and tubs. Shops on adjoining blocks sold cosmetics, combs, books and towels. At the front of many shops, a wooden plaque announced the establishment's name and specialty. Outside others, a fabric banner advertised its wares. The scent of freshly cut hinoki cypress emerged from an interior stocked with wooden cooking implements, joining with the fragrance of incense burning in a neighboring establishment and the aroma of roasted barley tea being brewed elsewhere nearby. Pots clanged, dogs barked and proprietors called out, hawking their goods for sale.

"Get your tobacco. And your pipes," one saleslady sang out.

"Woven hats, brooms and baskets," intoned a second woman.

"We got knifes and cleavers," declared a third.

On both sides of the roadway, customers milled around outside the shops, peering in at the merchandise. In one direction, the street advanced westward, cutting a straight line through the market district. In the other direction, the street ran several blocks toward the bridge spanning the Kamo River. People crammed together, watching comic and raunchy entertainments on the dry riverbed, where men had set up temporary stages. Farther on still was a streak of blue, the shallow water flowing under the bridge.

A fishmonger came trotting past the monkey trainer, yelling, "Fresh sea bream! Fresh mackerel!" The fishmonger had hoisted a long pole over one shoulder. Suspended from the pole in front of him was a wicker basket stacked with a mound of glistening seafood. Piled in a second basket at the rear was more fish. The pole arched under the weight of the baskets, which bounced and swayed with the vendor's quick steps.

From behind the fishmonger, a boy in a tattered smock jumped out, exposing two skinny legs with knobby knees. In a flash, the vendor was in the air, crying out, "Aghh!" His seafood flew helter-skelter and, as he landed on the pavement, fish came plummeting down around him. It hit the cobblestones in a series of wet thuds.

The lad pushed people out of his way and, dashing off, knocked a steely-haired woman against a stall. "Watch out!" he screamed with dust flying up at his heels. In an instant, he had turned down an alley and was gone.

With all the commotion, no one paid much attention to a solitary figure in dark garments entering the scene. It was a lanky fellow with a broad hat made from thin strips of bamboo, tightly woven and lacquered black. The hat, shaped like a volcanic dome, had a brim so wide it was impossible to make out the fellow's features—other than his strong chin, that is.

The fellow's hands were hidden under the front of a jacket dyed hunter green. He rested his forearms on two sword scabbards jutting out in front of his torso. One sword was long and the other short. The fellow had positioned the weapons at the ready, tucked under the sash wrapped around his hips.

Moving forward with a steady gait, the fellow stared down at the crushed stone on the road three steps ahead of him. Everything about the fellow spoke of a calculated control, excepting the strands of dark hair at his neck that flowed freely with each stride he took.

When the fellow reached the end of the block, a howl rose up from a storefront behind him. It came from the embellished doorway of an elegant shop known for purveying the finest steel blades in the old capital. The proprietor came charging out of the shop entrance. Portly and splendidly dressed, he quickly skirted around the fishmonger, now crawling on his hands and knees retrieving his seafood.

The proprietor looked around, pointed down the street and bellowed, "That rogue stole two of my best swords!"

Passersby froze in place, mouths agape.

"Stop him!" the proprietor yelled, his face flaming and his fists churning the air. "That man with the two swords—don't let him get away."

Now a younger man emerged from the sword shop. A junior clerk, he darted around the proprietor and scanned the street. Spotting the fellow with the stolen swords more than a block away, he took off in pursuit, shouting, "You! Stop right there."

The fellow in the hat had been casually retreating, but now he halted with his back to the clerk, a powerful tension in his pose.

After sprinting down the block, the clerk slowed a few storefronts away from his target and pulled out a dagger. Onlookers backed up to clear the way for the clerk.

The fellow in the hat turned to face the clerk with a look of scorn. He withdrew his right arm from under his robe and lifted his hand holding a large hunting knife by its blade.

The clerk stopped. He pointed his dagger. Then he sprang forward.

In a flash, the fellow in the hat flung his hunting knife. The blade curved through the air like a gleaming ribbon—a graceful extension of his arm. The blade hit its target with deadly accuracy, lodging in the clerk's chest.

The clerk stepped back onto one foot. His right eye twitched. His head bobbed. He let out a "Gyaaah" and toppled over in the street, where he groaned twice and fell utterly still.

The shop proprietor came running. He stumbled, fell to his knees next to the clerk and shuddered.

A hush descended across the bystanders as everything came to a standstill—except the fellow in the hat, who was moving at a fast clip away from the body of the lifeless clerk. The fellow traversed two blocks and slipped away, disappearing down a side street.

Hunched over his slain employee, the shop proprietor expelled several long sobs. Then he reached out and pulled the hunting knife from his clerk's chest. Lifting his head, he howled, "It was that rōnin Kurōbei! You saw what he did! He killed Sōsuke! Kurōbei cut down my shop assistant in broad daylight—murdered him in cold blood."

The proprietor rose up. Facing the direction in which the fellow in the black hat had vanished, the proprietor shook a fist in the air and roared, "You'll pay for this, you lawless thief. I'll see to it—even if I have to go to Edo and seek justice from the shōgun. You're a curse on us all, Ishida Kurōbei."

"We're almost there," declared Deputy Inspector Tanaka Taisuke, his voice deep and penetrating even out on the busy street.

"Yes, sir," responded the two agents flanking him.

Compact and composed, Tanaka was a ranking investigator in the Office of the Kyoto Governor, the bureau charged with enforcing laws written by shogunal leaders far off in Edo. On a morning patrol, Tanaka was leading his agents through a northern district of the old capital. The three were heading toward the open grounds where two of Kyoto's main waterways, the Takano River and the Kamo River, converged.

Having just left behind the western wall of an aristocratic estate, Tanaka and his agents took their time strolling down the sunny street. Like his agents, Tanaka moved with a swagger, wearing a laborer's dusty old clothes, a heavy apron and a roughly-woven bamboo hat. This was a departure from Tanaka's usual immaculate grooming and formal bearing.

"It's steamy already. Mushiatsui," observed The Crab, named for his broad, bumpy forehead. He was small and the youngest of the three men.

"Yup. Hot," agreed The Wolf. Strong and sinewy, The Wolf's shaggy hair was hanging in loose clumps.

The deputy inspector acknowledged his agents' observations with a crisp nod and a "Hm."

Reaching their destination, Tanaka left the roadway and took respite in the shade under a leafy ginko tree. The agents followed.

"At least we're out of the sun. Ugh," groaned The Crab loudly. His irritable tone was part of his disguise. Normally, he wouldn't dare speak so coarsely within earshot of his superior, the deputy inspector.

"And there's a gentle breeze coming off the river," noted The Wolf.

The three men stood side by side facing east. Despite the obscuring effect of a heat haze, they could see for miles. First, they took in the impressive view of Mount Hiei to the left and then the rolling eastern foothills directly across town from where they stood.

After several minutes, Tanaka pivoted to observe pedestrians. The two agents also turned to face west.

In a low voice, The Crab asked his boss, "Who's at the top of your wanted list this week, sir?"

Tanaka responded without hesitation. "Ishida Kurōbei."

"Sir, you think he's the one who stole the two swords and killed the shop clerk yesterday?" inquired The Crab, still speaking softly.

"I suspect so. He fits the description—" Tanaka held off, seeing a team of construction workers approaching from the north. They were hauling a cart stacked with lumber, and they were talking loudly enough for Tanaka and his agents to hear.

"That's not my favorite stall. That's *your's*," declared one of the carters.

"Because their noodles taste better," replied his fellow carter.

"No, they don't!" argued the first.

"Yes, they do."

Tanaka watched out the corner of one eye as the team continued on, moving their cart farther down the road.

When the cart was gone, The Wolf spoke up, inquiring of his boss, "Did you recognize those men, sir?"

"Yes. They're working with carpenters to restore buildings on the palace grounds."

"The buildings destroyed two years ago, sir?" asked The Crab. "In the palace fire set by those two girls?"

Tanaka nodded, still observing foot traffic and watching for any sign of a problem.

Now, a pair of beefy men appeared, one with a folded tarp strapped to his back, and the other with a rug slung over one shoulder. Heading southward, the pair tramped wordlessly past Tanaka and his agents.

Once they were out of sight, The Wolf remarked, "Those two must be heading downtown to help with preparations for the Gion Festival."

"Workers are setting up already?" inquired The Crab.

Tanaka nodded.

"Say, did I tell you?" The Crab interjected. "My nephew will help tow one of the huge floats in the closing procession—the one with the warrior monk from the old story."

The Wolf glanced at his fellow agent, asking, "The story of Benkei on the Bridge?"

"Yup." The Crab answered and guffawed. "Ha! I feel sorry for the kid playing the young hero. He's got to hold his toy sword and stand on one foot while the float lurches forward."

Tanaka became silent again, now focusing his attention on a small group of spectators in an empty lot nearby. The spectators were applauding a tall young fellow, who had just taken a bow. Despite the heat, the young performer was wearing dark leggings and a long-sleeve hemp jacket with a pine needle design. A portable sign identified him as an unemployed, masterless warrior asking for a few coins in exchange for his display of skill with a sword. According to the sign, the rōnin swordsman had been trained by an instructor in the employ of a relative of the Tokugawa shōgun.

Tanaka and his agents watched as the performer began brandishing his weapon.

"He moves nimbly enough," remarked The Crab.

"But he lacks skill with his sword," The Wolf observed.

"And he's impulsive," stated the deputy inspector.

After several minutes, Tanaka made a quick hand gesture, signaling that it was time for them to get moving. "Return here in an hour," Tanaka ordered.

The trio turned their backs on the swordsman and strode off, each heading in a different direction. They would conduct their regular morning patrol, examining exteriors of residences and offices. Checking with guards at front entrances and servants at side exits, they would inquire whether strangers had been seen loitering around or whether any unusual incidents had occurred.

Tanaka, responsible for patrolling a neighborhood of aristocratic residences near the imperial palace, marched west for five minutes. When he arrived at a quiet intersection with tall whitewashed walls on each corner, he took a left. Moving southward, the deputy inspector followed one of the walls of the Nijō estate, home to a leading aristocrat. Not only was the current head of the Nijō family married to the retired emperor's daughter, but he had recently been appointed imperial regent.

Tanaka turned again and advanced toward the Nijō gate, where a guard stood erect with his feet planted on a large paving stone. The deputy inspector stopped to exchange a daily greeting with the guard.

The guard addressed him warmly. "Good day, Deputy Inspector Tanaka. How are things today?"

"All's well," answered Tanaka with a dip of his head. "Anything to report this morning?"

"No, sir. Nothing out of the ordinary."

"Excellent. Then I won't keep you. Take care of yourself in this heat."

"Of course, sir. You take care, as well." The guard bowed.

With that, Tanaka turned away from the Nijō gate and resumed his route, moving on to the next mansion.

AKI'S LESSON

What's it all about? Aki asked herself.

The sixteen-year old had just left her home, a thatched hut tucked away among the tall pines far to the north on Kyoto's eastern slopes. Aki had the soft, smooth skin and the round cheeks of a girl, but she was old enough to be a wife and a mother. In fact, most local women her age were married, some already expecting a child.

On her way for a lesson at the convent of Enshōji, Aki moved swiftly, eager to ask her teacher about something she'd overheard at the market the previous day. Several men had been grumbling about the rōnin problem. Aki wasn't sure what they were referring to, but she felt sure her teacher could tell her more.

Branches shifted in the breeze and birds chattered away, ignoring the young woman passing below through patches of sunlight. Aki continued downhill, keeping her eyes on the trail to avoid tree roots and half-buried rocks. When she finally glanced up from the path, she saw the edge of the forest just ahead. Beyond were terraced fields and thatched farmhouses. A few weeks earlier, when shoots were emerging, the fields had looked like pale green carpets. Now, the rice plants would reach above her ankles if she were to walk across one of those fields.

A bit farther on, Aki noticed three women coming her way, carrying bags of dirty clothing to wash and mend. She recognized them as farmers' wives from the nearby village.

"Here comes Aki—acting like a refined lady. Ha, ha!" blurted out the tallest of the women, loudly enough for Aki to hear.

The shortest of them added, "Ha! Look at that silly get up of hers!"

Aki was wearing the grey robe and brown sash that her teacher had given her several months earlier. She had tied her hair back and secured it with a bit of cord at the nape of her neck to keep it from falling forward as she bent over her desk for a lesson.

"That's Miss Aki's uniform. She's learning to read at the convent," commented Inu, daughter of the village headman. Inu was younger than her companions, about the same age as Aki.

Inu's taller companion laughed again. "Ha, ha! Aki thinks she's special because she visits the convent. But she's no different from us."

Sneering, the short woman added, "Just like casting pearls to pigs. Buta ni shinju."

"What!" Aki had been planning to step aside for the women to pass, but hearing their taunts, she stopped, blocking their way.

As the women halted, Inu quickly set down her sack of laundry. Stretching her arms out to hold back her companions, Inu warned them, "Hush up, you two." Then turning back to Aki, Inu mumbled in a conciliatory tone, "Please excuse us, Miss Aki. We're just common village women. We aren't educated."

Her expression softening, Aki remarked, "I understand, Miss Inu." Aki dipped her head, stepped away and continued on past the women.

With that, Inu picked up her laundry and, heading uphill, called out, "Goodbye, Miss Aki."

The other two remained where they were, however. The shorter one turned toward Aki's back and jeered, "Just wait until they see that blood mark of yours!"

The two women snickered. "Heh, heh, heh."

Stung, Aki pictured the deep red birthmark that ran down the middle of her chest. The mark was shaped like the written character shi, meaning death.

Never mind, Aki said to herself without looking back. They're just jealous. They pretend to be satisfied working the fields and doing others' laundry, but I know better. They wish they could study at Enshōji, too. I'm the one learning things. And I'm going to learn as much as Sister Bunkai will teach me.

It took a while, but Aki finally got the taunts out of her head. When she arrived at a spot where the trees and bushes parted, she stopped and moved to one side of the path to gaze over the farms of Shugakuin.

My mom and I *do* belong here, Aki thought. We might be different from the others, but this is *our* home, too.

After moving on, Aki caught sight ahead of the tiled roofs of Enshōji above the tree line. There were hundreds of Buddhist temples and convents in the ancient capital, but Enshōji was special. An imperial convent, it was dedicated to the teachings of Rinzai Zen. Moreover, it was run by a former princess. The abbess of Enshōji, known as Daitsū Bunchi, was the eldest sister of the emperor. Fourteen years earlier, she had selected Shugakuin as the site of her imperial convent and, once the new buildings were finished, Bunchi had moved in.

Within minutes, Aki was walking through the side gate of the convent. Just ahead, at the far side of the compound, three kitchen nuns busied themselves with outdoor chores. A burly, middle-aged man with a dark complexion emerged from behind one of several convent structures. He was the manservant of Enshōji, the only male living on the premises. He protected the residents, announced visitors, received deliveries and cleaned the grounds.

"Hello, Miss Yamanaka," the manservant called out, making his way toward Aki.

Aki lowered her head and returned his greeting. "Good morning, sir."

"It's turning into a fine day. Ii tenki desu ne?"

"It is," Aki replied.

"She's waiting for you at the Ryokuin'an," the manservant stated.

Aki knew the manservant was referring to Kūgon Bunkai, a nun at the convent and her teacher. Thanking the man, Aki turned and walked across the grounds. Ahead, she caught sight of a petite woman standing on a raised wooden veranda encircling the Ryokuin'an subtemple. It was Bunkai with her shaved head and nun's habit. Waving and smiling, Bunkai rose up onto her tiptoes, gesturing for Aki to hurry.

Bunkai was a mature woman ten years older than Aki, but she looked like a porcelain doll, at least that's what Aki thought. When Aki had first met Bunkai, several years earlier, she'd presumed that the nun was rather delicate. She'd come to realize, however, that Bunkai was robust and full of energy.

Aki greeted her teacher with a bow. "Good morning, Sister Bunkai."

"Are you ready?" asked the nun.

"Uh, huh," replied Aki as she bent down to remove her straw sandals. Once barefoot, she climbed the steps to the veranda and followed the nun through the doorway.

Inside, Bunkai made her way to the larger of two desks. She lowered herself onto a flat, square cushion meant for sitting and pointed toward a handscroll on the smaller desk near the doorway. She said, "I chose a sutra passage for you to transcribe today, Aki."

Aki went to the desk and, tucking her feet beneath her, she sat on a cushion of her own. She leaned forward to examine the scroll. It consisted of many sheets of paper glued together to form a long horizontal surface. Columns of calligraphy covered the scroll. Aki recognized these as lines from a Buddhist scripture. She could read some of the text, but not all of it.

Setting to work, Aki made a puddle of ink and grabbed a sheet of paper from a stack at her left. She laid the sheet down on her desk next to the scriptural passage. Then, she selected a writing brush from a cylindrical container beside the ink-stone. She dipped the pliant tip of the brush in the ink and began her transcription, attempting to imitate the scriptural text as closely as possible. After a long stretch of quiet concentration, Aki glanced up at her teacher, who was busy reading.

Without looking up, Bunkai adjusted her position, sitting even straighter than before. Then she lifted her head and let out a soft sigh, saying, "Do you have a question, Aki?"

"Yes. Why does Abbess Bunchi allow me study here, Sister Bunkai?"

Bunkai paused before answering. "The reverend mother told me she wants you to learn how to read and write."

"Yes, but I'm a commoner, and this is an imperial convent."

"I'm sure I told you the reverend mother's thoughts about this, Aki."

"Yes, you did," Aki replied, going on to repeat what the nun had told her some time ago. "The abbess made an exception in my case. Usually, she maintains strict rules for members of the Enshōji community. Those at lower levels don't interact much with those above."

Bunkai nodded, adding, "At many other convents, rules are less stringently enforced. But our regulations at Enshōji allow us to live in harmony."

"My mother explained all that to me," Aki remarked. "She said she respects the Enshōji abbess for following monastic regulations so closely. But why does Abbess Bunchi permit *me* to attend the prayer sessions? I haven't taken the precepts. Did the abbess tell you I don't need to follow the rules?"

Bunkai shot Aki a warning glance, saying, "No. The reverend mother wants you to learn about life at the convent and about her family."

"And I'm glad she does, Sister Bunkai. I want to learn everything."

"You do? Ha!" Bunkai gave a little chuckle. "Do you want to be called a walking dictionary like me?"

"Why not! You don't mind it. Do you, Sister Bunkai?"

Bunkai's eyebrows shot up, but she answered calmly, "I don't. But knowing names and places doesn't help a person gain true insight, Aki."

"Still, I think it's great to know a lot." Aki paused and abruptly changed the subject, continuing to probe and still hoping to learn something new. "Sister Bunkai, are the masterless warriors having a hard time?"

"The rōnin?" Bunkai responded in surprise.

"Uh, huh. I heard someone say the rōnin are struggling."

"Hmm," Bunkai muttered. "I suppose the rōnin *are* struggling. But where to start?"

"So what if those men don't have a lord to serve? I realize people think it's a problem, but why?"

"Are you playing dumb again, Aki?" answered Bunkai. "I'm sure you know that when a lord loses his lands, his warrior retainers are dispossessed. They have to make their way in the world on their own. Some end up penniless. In a few cases, the rōnin become desperate and decide to act."

"So, what do they do?" Aki queried, even though she already had a good idea.

Bunkai glanced back at her student, who had planted one elbow on her desk, resting her chin in her cupped palm and listening closely.

Bunkai shook her head and went on. "Well, I suppose you've heard that one group of rōnin in the new capital planned to attack Edo Castle and stage the Edo Insurrection of 1651—"

Aki interrupted. "I heard they plotted to assassinate the Tokugawa shōgun and kill his top advisors, but police stopped them. Is that true?"

Frowning, Bunkai replied, "It is."

"Why would masterless warriors want to kill the shōgun?"

Instead of answering, Bunkai looked off into a corner of the study.

"Those men must have been monsters," Aki stated. "But I've heard people say other rōnin aren't so bad."

With a look of resignation, Bunkai adjusted the front collar of her habit and remarked, "I'm sure they're right, Aki. But many rōnin are truly unhappy."

"Unhappy?"

"Yes," answered the nun before going on to explain. "When I was younger, some masterless warriors were able to find employment as guards or mercenaries. But men trained for war were no longer in great demand. So, there's been much suffering among the masterless warriors, in Edo and elsewhere."

"I see," Aki mumbled.

"Many rōnin employed in towns have been accused of wrongdoing," Bunkai remarked. "They've been blamed for starting brawls on city streets and frequenting gambling dens. In the countryside, rōnin working the fields have been accused of inciting uprisings. But those men are struggling. Some can't feed their families. You might be surprised to learn, Aki, that many of the masterless warriors are well educated. Some even study Chinese ethics."

Standing abruptly, the nun crossed her study, moving toward a set of shoji doors. She slid open one door to reveal a narrow garden where ornamental rocks had been carefully placed and shrubs had been laboriously pruned to look like a small version of an expansive landscape. The nun remained there, looking abstractly into the garden.

Aki realized her teacher wanted to drop the subject of masterless warriors, and so she quietly resumed her transcription.

"THOSE INSECTS ARE DEAFENING TONIGHT," MUTTERED ONE OF two sentries guarding the Katō estate, nestled in the eastern foothills of the old capital.

The colleague, shorter but just as muscular, agreed. "Sure are! What a racket! Koro koro, koro koro."

The two had been hired by Katō Gosaemon, scion of a wealthy Kyoto family. Gosaemon had ordered the sentries to remain on guard throughout the night, informing them that the safety of his family was at stake.

"The master here—his family has been in the saké brewing business for some time?" asked the first sentry.

"Yup. For decades," his colleague replied, before turning and marching off.

The crickets droned on as the sentries moved back and forth across the grounds. The half moon in the clear, dark sky illuminated a picturesque pond, a manicured garden and a cluster of buildings.

The sentries had been patrolling the Katō precinct for several hours already, each equipped with a sword and a dagger. During the first quarter hour, they had taken up positions in the central yard. Next, they stationed themselves at the perimeter, one at the north and the other at the south. They walked up and back, scanning the walls. Then the pair halted and signaled to one another from across the small pond. Each man raised his hand to his brow, silently communicating an all's well. After repeating the sequence seven times, the sentries marched to the middle of the compound, where they met again.

"It's dead quiet—shiin," reported the first sentry.

"No threat detected," confirmed his colleague.

The guards' employer had warned them that a dangerous thief was on the loose. They knew exactly who he was. For days now, people across town had been hearing his name—Ishida Kurōbei. Several days earlier, Kurōbei had snatched two expensive swords from a renowned downtown shop and, when the clerk had chased after him to retrieve the blades, Kurōbei had cut him down. Scores of pedestrians had witnessed the murder in broad daylight on a busy street.

"What time do you think it is?" inquired the first sentry.

"Midnight, maybe?" his shorter colleague replied.

"Smell that?" the first sentry asked.

"No. What?"

The first sentry lifted his nose and breathed deeply. "Gardenia."

"Oh!"

"So fragrant! It's coming from over there." The first sentry pointed to a shrub with white blossoms before taking a seat on a flat-topped rock nearby. "I'll keep watch from here for a while."

"Fine," his colleague stated. "I'll head toward the front gate."

The seated sentry began observing reflections undulating across the surface of the pond. After a short while, he turned his attention upward, staring at movements in the sky. A blanket of clouds came drifting in, consuming the moonlight and momentarily casting the garden into darkness. Gradually, a silver radiance began to illuminate the edges of the clouds. Just as the moonlight became bright enough for the seated sentry to make out features of the garden, the humming of the insects came to an abrupt halt.

As if from nowhere, a lanky male figure appeared at the far side of the garden behind the seated sentry. The figure began leaping from rock to rock and then to an earthen mound, stopping in a half-crouch. He called out sharply, "Hey, Mister. You, over there!"

The seated sentry froze. When it registered that there was a trespasser behind him, the sentry twisted around and shouted, "You! Stop right there!"

"Me?" asked the intruder, touching his chest with one finger. Then he lifted his two empty hands in the air.

The sentry now made out the intruder's high cheekbones, pinched nostrils and a ragged scar below his left temple. Caught in the moonlight, the intruder's face was contorted in a sneer.

The second guard came running up from the far side of the estate, yelling out, "Prowler on the grounds!"

Still squatting, the intruder cocked his head to the side, ignoring the approaching guard.

The guard charged forward, reaching for his sword. At lightening speed, he pulled out his weapon, grasped the hilt with both hands and pointed the blade upward.

The intruder stood, withdrew his own sword with a soft, scraping sound and faced the rushing guard. Once the guard was upon him, he swung his blade, making a "Hssih, swish." There was a blur of steel, and the intruder jumped from the mound, his blade leaving a deep, diagonal slash across the attacking guard's neck. Blood began shooting from the wound.

The guard quaked, took a step back and crumpled to the ground.

The intruder sprang to the side just as the other sentry came running up with a roar, his sword unsheathed. The clanging of blades announced a pitched struggle, accompanied by the sentry's cries and the intruder's laughter. Within seconds, the second sentry had also been struck down. There, in the moonlight on the white raked gravel of the garden of the Katō estate, he died.

Katō Gosaemon had been awakened and had jumped from his bed. Ordering his wife to stay inside and protect their children, he grabbed a dagger.

Gosaemon opened a door and silently stepped out onto the raised veranda. Much to his shock, he saw the bodies of his two sentries sprawled out in the yard below him.

Before he could compose his thoughts, Gosaemon's knees buckled. "Gyaaah," he cried out, hit by searing pain in his lower back.

The intruder had struck Gosaemon from behind.

Gosaemon dropped his weapon and fell onto the veranda deck.

"Where's your money?" growled the intruder.

Gosaemon stammered, "It's—it's in—"

"Speak up!" the intruder demanded.

"It's in the storehouse." Gosaemon pointed toward the opposite side of the residence.

"Get the key!"

Gosaemon rolled over and stood with a groan. "Aghh."

The intruder grabbed Gosaemon's robe at the nape of his neck and pushed, forcing him to move. Gosaemon limped forward.

After locating the key, Gosaemon opened the heavy iron lock securing the storehouse door. Only then did he catch a glimpse of his assailant's form. As the moon emerged from behind the clouds, a cold light fell on the criminal's face and revealed his features, including a scar shaped like a bolt of lightning.

The intruder struck Gosaemon again, this time across the back of his head. Gosaemon collapsed.

*　　*　　*

When he regained consciousness, Katō Gosaemon was laying in his bed. Members of his family were sitting alongside him, and several strangers were nearby. Two of the strangers introduced themselves as agents of the Kyoto police.

"You're lucky," one of the agents told Gosaemon. "You survived."

"What's that?" Gosaemon mumbled incoherently.

"A thief attacked you, Mister Katō."

Gosaemon reached up and touched his forehead, which was wrapped in a bandage. He winced.

"The thief killed your two guards. He stole the money in your storehouse."

In his foggy state, Gosaemon took a few minutes to process what he was being told. Then an image flashed in his head. The intruder's scar. It was the last thing Gosaemon remembered seeing before the blow that knocked him out.

Finally, after it all sank in, Gosaemon managed to speak, even though his throat was dry and his voice cracked. Gosaemon had a question for the policemen.

"The thief—who was he?" Gosaemon asked.

"It was that rōnin outlaw."

"Ah!" Gosaemon responded, not at all surprised.

"He calls himself Shining Blade," the policeman clarified. "His real name is Ishida Kurōbei."

Gosaemon sucked in his breath weakly. "Kurōbei!"

"Don't worry, sir," said the policeman. "Deputy Inspector Tanaka will hear about this immediately. He'll track Kurōbei down."

"Bye, mom," Aki called out.

"Beware the slippery spots on the trail!" Natsu warned, watching her daughter pass through the gate at the edge of their yard.

Aki set off downhill on the steep footpath. In her indigo jacket, tan leggings and straw sandals, Aki looked like other firewood carriers on the slopes of Mount Hiei. Draped over her head was a brown scarf, the two ends of which touched her shoulders. Atop her head was a round padded cushion, protecting her scalp from the sharp ends of twigs sticking out of the kindling.

Aki was on her way to deliver firewood bundles to three aristrocratic residences in Kyoto, just as she did most mornings. Even though the heavy bundles bore down on her neck, Aki walked at a fast clip, hoping to complete her deliveries and return home before noon.

Aki gave the impression of having a mild temperament and a calm disposition. Concentrating on her steps, she loosened her jaw with her lips parted. Suddenly, however, she felt the tip of her right sandal catch on a protruding root. Lurching forward, Aki let out a cry, "Agh!"

Slamming down her left foot, Aki tried to steady herself, but her sandal slid across moss and mud. As her knees began to buckle, Aki's hands shot up, and she clutched at the bundles of kindling on her head. She pictured herself pitching head over heels down the embankment, her firewood scattering around her.

Automatically bending her knees, Aki tensed her belly. She planted her two feet on solid ground and quickly regained control. She adjusted the kindling on her head and breathed deeply. I'm fine, she told herself. No problem.

Aki glanced down the narrow trail snaking out of the foothills, and, as she started walking again, she considered what lay ahead. I suppose I'll get sweaty on my deliveries again today. But I better get used to that. It's the rainy season now. Too bad my deliveries require me to be covered head to toe.

Noticing that the path was leveling off and the surrounding undergrowth thinning, Aki glanced to her right, where a vista of Shugakuin appeared. Sunlight flooded down and reflected off the earthen walls of scattered barns, each with a thick layer of thatch on its roof. Continuing on a bit farther, Aki spied figures in the distance trudging across a short bridge spanning the Otowa River. It was the first of many bridges Aki would cross that morning.

Before long, Aki was following a crew of laborers onto the bridge. As usual, she slowed to peer down into the rushing waters. Then, leaving the river behind, Aki turned and headed in a direction different from the crew, entering a short stretch of empty lane. Another few minutes, and she heard distant hammering coming from a wooded lot ahead.

Aki recalled her teacher, Sister Bunkai, saying that construction had started on a great temple there. An imperial abbot was overseeing development of a new home on the site. Sister Bunkai had told her that the only parts completed so far were a simple bamboo fence and a temporary brushwood gate, but splendid buildings and gardens were being planned for the compound.

Wondering what it looked like, Aki decided to stop and sneak into the precinct. She moved to the side of the lane across from the brushwood gate. She knelt behind a section of fence, lifted the kindling from her head and set the bundles on the ground where they'd be hidden and safe. She shrugged her shoulders and, as she started stretching her neck to one side, she heard voices.

Aki leaned forward and peered through a gap in the bamboo slats of the fence. She saw two men approaching, caught up in conversation. One of the men wore long-sleeved satin robes dyed pale violet. The other had plainer garments, a white robe under a starched, black jacket with a gossamer weave. The latter had the fully shaved head of a priest.

Oh! Gentlemen from the imperial court, Aki realized. Confident the two men couldn't see her, she remained kneeling and watched closely. They were near enough now for Aki to hear.

"What they've done is intolerable!" complained the gentleman in the violet robe. He bent forward slightly, his torso seeming to hold a coiled-up tension.

His companion, the priest, nodded quietly, his expression troubled.

Coming to a sudden stop, the gentleman in violet knitted his brow and declared, "The government puts the screws to those miserable rōnin. Hidoi!"

Aki pressed her lips together, worried she might blurt something out involuntarily—like a question.

The priest, who had also halted, added his own lament, saying, "I feel so sorry for warriors who've lost their masters. Let's hope none of them approach his majesty beseeching him for support."

"Indeed!" The gentleman in violet agreed, pausing for a moment before he resumed his harangue. "And the shōgun forced the emperor to marry his daughter—what arrogance!"

Agreeing, the priest shook his head, mumbling, "But—"

His companion interrupted to say, "It's just preposterous to think that girls started that palace fire last year. Do you think it's possible those lies were spread by government spies?"

"Well—" the priest paused, tilting his head to one side and looking chagrined.

The gentleman in violet scowled, adding, "And I'm sure you've heard—Edo refused the emperor's request to train with a sword. What's next? Will someone try to kidnap the emperor?"

Aki's head jerked back involuntarily. Fortunately, she was still hidden behind the fence and hadn't made a sound.

"We must do something," the gentleman in violet demanded.

The priest cleared his throat and answered in a mild tone. "I agree. For now, though, let's have a quick look around the temple grounds. Then we can return to the palace." He guided his companion to the right, leading the way through the brushwood gate.

As the men moved off, Aki remained squatting behind the fence. Bamboo leaves rustled nearby, responding to a slight gust of wind. The edge of Aki's headscarf brushed against her cheek. A yellow butterfly descended and perched on a rock.

A nagging sensation registered. Aki realized it was the stinging of pebbles pressing through her leggings, imbedding themselves into her knee.

I've got to get going, Aki realized. Standing, she brushed the pebbles from her knee and adjusted her wrist coverings. She stepped out from behind the fence, hoisted the kindling back onto her head and returned to the road, forgetting that she had planned to sneak onto the temple grounds. She set off for Shirakawa Avenue.

* * *

"The heat and humidity ganged up on us today," muttered Aki's mother, Natsu.

Aki nodded without looking up.

It was late afternoon, and Aki was sitting with her mother. They were winding balls of twine in the yard outside their mountain hut.

A stranger might not guess the two were mother and daughter. While Natsu had long legs and straight hair, Aki was rather short with a wavy mane. Natsu's face was narrow and her nose prominent, whereas Aki's face was round and her nose small, making her appear younger than her age. Natsu always kept her head up as a result of carrying a basket of flowers on her head, but when she was tired, she walked with a slight limp, evidence of an injury she had suffered years earlier. Aki, on the other hand, looked robust as she charged forward with kindling on her head, moving with her center of gravity low to the ground.

"I thought I'd be able to sell all my flowers today, but one was left over." Natsu gestured toward a small ceramic cylinder on the table next to the outdoor chopping block. The cylinder held a stem of blue hydrangea in full bloom.

Natsu was a Shirakawa flower lady. Every morning, she walked downhill to the Shirakawa market, picked up seasonal blooms from a supplier, set the flowers in a basket and lifted the basket onto her head. Then she carried the flowers into town and began her route, walking the streets as she called out her items for sale.

"Mom—" Aki hesitated and looked down. She tapped her clogs together for a moment before adding, "Something happened today."

"What? Dō shita no?" asked Natsu, her thin eyebrows nearly merging as she furrowed her brow.

"Well, I was passing by the entrance to the new temple. You know, the one near the Otowa River. Two men showed up. They were talking—" Aki paused before plunging ahead, still avoiding her mother's gaze. "One of the men must be an important person at the emperor's court. He said the shōgun had treated the emperor badly. The shōgun made the emperor marry his daughter, and the warriors who've lost their masters are miserable and the emperor might be abducted."

Aki looked over, noticing Natsu's expression. It conveyed none of the casual restraint Aki was accustomed to. Her mother's cheeks, usually ruddy from the sun, had turned pale. And something had tightened on her face.

"What's it all mean, mom?" Aki asked innocently.

"You listened in on a private conversation, Aki?"

"I wasn't eavesdropping, mom. I mean, those men didn't see me, and I didn't want to interrupt them. So, I ducked behind a fence."

Natsu's tone turned accusatory as she declared, "You've been sneaking around, trying to learn people's secrets!"

"No, mom. I haven't," Aki answered defensively. "I just happened to overhear them."

"Listen, Aki. I'll say it again—it's wrong to spread rumors. And it's dangerous to gossip about people. You're a grown-up woman now. You're sixteen years old. Act your age!"

Aki dropped her head. She felt her face burning.

Still reproving her daughter, Natsu added, "You'll get yourself in trouble one day, Aki."

Aki couldn't ignore her mother's severe tone. She stayed silent, staring at her own feet.

"You have a lot to lose, Aki. Don't you realize how fortunate you are? You're studying with a respected nun at an imperial convent. You know perfectly well that Kūgon Bunkai was once in service to the former empress and that her mother is a trusted associate of the Enshōji abbess."

Aki nodded.

"It's extremely rare for a young woman living in a mountain hut to have the opportunity to learn to read and write. The Enshōji nuns treat you with extreme kindness, Aki. But if you're not trustworthy and if you cause trouble, they'll put an end to your studies. They'll be forced to."

Aki nodded again.

"Let me remind you of a wise saying—the less you know, the safer you'll be," Natsu added. With that, she stood and headed into the hut, leaving her daughter alone in the yard.

Aki remained seated, wondering what had made her mother lash out. She's being too harsh, Aki thought. It's not fair.

Gradually, Aki's thoughts returned to the two gentlemen she'd overheard that morning. It's not my fault they were speaking so loudly, Aki thought. But why was the gentleman in violet so upset?

Maybe Sister Bunkai can tell me more. I'll ask her when I see her for my next lesson, Aki decided. Ugh, I hate waiting!

"Where is he?" snarled the tall fellow. Wearing dark leggings and a jacket with a pine needle design in green, he had a pinched nose and a scar on his temple. It was Ishida Kurōbei.

Standing alone outside a market in the First Street Temple district, Kurōbei was expecting a new recruit to show up across the street at the market's front entrance. In his right hand, he held a short willow branch, which he slapped against the wall behind him. He turned his head to peer left and then right.

It was a mild, overcast morning in northeastern Kyoto. Sounds of merchants and laborers echoed through the neighborhood.

After a few minutes, Kurōbei tossed his branch aside and placed his hands on his hips. He started shifting his weight from one foot to the other. Everything about him spoke of aggravation.

A spare, young man emerged from the far end of the lane and hurried toward Kurōbei. Stopping a few feet away, he lowered his head and blurted out a greeting. "Good morning, Master Ishida. I'm ready to start training with a sword."

"It's about time," Kurōbei snapped. "Tell me—are you still committed to the rōnin cause?"

"Yes, sir. I hope to receive instruction in the art of sword fighting."

Kurōbei grunted in response. "Hm! Let's go!" He set off, clenching his fists as he strode forward, leading the aspiring trainee through side streets.

Kurōbei had met the younger fellow several weeks earlier. One of his father's former colleagues—a likeminded rōnin—had backed the fellow's request to join Kurōbei's underground movement. Kurōbei had grilled the aspiring trainee on his family, his skills, his education and his views.

As the two men moved rapidly eastward, the number of buildings nearby diminished and the uphill path narrowed. Soon they arrived at a large, run-down barn, clearly abandoned long ago.

Kurōbei pushed open a low wooden gate, stepped into the yard and entered the barn. The aspiring recruit followed him into a spacious interior, which had been cleared and its earthen floor swept. Light filtered through gaps in the boarded roof. A row of burlap mannequins stuffed with straw leaned against one wall. Three archery targets attached to bales of hay hugged another wall.

From the shadows, two men emerged to greet Kurōbei. They wore training garments, one in dark maroon and the other in a soft tawny brown.

Kurōbei told the aspiring recruit, "These men will instruct you. They are expert swordsmen."

"Yes, sir," the fellow replied.

Turning to the instructors, Kurōbei stated, "Time to demonstrate your skills."

The instructors bowed toward Kurōbei and headed to a rack at the opposite side of the barn, where they each picked up a wooden practice blade. Returning to the center of the barn, they faced one another and bowed. They raised their weapon, planted their feet firmly with knees bent and commenced. As the instructors began to move laterally, each extended his blade forward.

Kurōbei narrated the action. "Maneuvers are generally slow and calculated, but attacks must be performed swiftly. And accurately. You will learn."

The would-be recruit nodded, eagerly.

The sparring entailed a lengthy sequence of moves. The instructors each took a careful step toward the right, then another. Suddenly, the instructor in maroon lunged, his wooden sword outstretched at waist height. The man in brown jumped back, avoiding his opponent's reach.

"That's the thrust. It's one way to attack," Kurōbei explained. "If you're fighting with a steel sword, you place the sharp edge in one of four positions—up, down, left, or right."

The instructors now assumed another stance. They lowered their wooden swords so the tips pointed toward the ground.

The instructor in brown took a quick step to the left and swept his weapon upward. This time it was the instructor in maroon jumping back to avoid being struck.

As Kurōbei continued, his face remained expressionless, but his eyes shone brightly. "Another way to attack the enemy is with a slicing movement of the sword. Slashing upward from below can be highly effective. The blade gathers momentum. It's not easy for the opponent to block a slash like that, especially if the sharper edge of the blade is facing up."

Now the pair of instructors moved apart, maintaining fighting stances. They continued taking deliberate steps toward the right or the left, and occasionally forward. The instructor in brown griped the hilt of his wooden sword with one hand and placed his other palm along the back ridge of his weapon. The instructor in maroon responded by grabbing his wooden sword with a two-handed grip.

"As you see, there are a variety of hand positions and arm movements a fighter can choose. But you'll need to learn a great deal more than how to handle a weapon. You must master strategies."

The aspiring recruit confirmed his willingness.

"Hm!" Kurōbei responded, calling out to the two instructors. "That's enough!"

The two men ceased their sparing and returned their wooden swords to the racks. Making their way to the far side of the barn, they squatted on their haunches.

Kurōbei paused and narrowed his eyes at the would-be recruit. "You will need to train here every day. It will require absolute discipline," Kurōbei declared, elaborating on what would be expected of the recruit in terms of vigor and perseverance. He told the fellow that training would be tough.

Once Kurōbei had determined that the fellow seemed, at first blush, to meet his requirements for new recruits, he faced the newcomer and asked him directly, "Will you devote yourself to perfection of body and mind?"

"Yes, sir." The fellow nodded. "I will, sir."

Kurōbei stepped back, assuming his full height with his posture erect and his chin raised. He glowered down at the fellow. A hissing sound came from his lips as he sucked in his breath.

At last, Kurōbei withdrew his gaze from the recruit, stating, "Alright then. Return here tomorrow at sunrise. Wear training gear and be ready to spend the day drilling. Understood?"

"Yes, sir. Thank you very much, sir." The recruit bent at the waist in a deep bow.

"Fine—now go. I'm busy."

Still bending forward, the young man backed up several steps. Then he straightened, turned and left.

The barn grew still with Kurōbei standing in the middle of the training floor, scowling.

AKI TELLS BUNKAI ABOUT THE TWO GENTLEMEN

"START ON YOUR LESSON," SAID THE NUN, SITTING AND READING at her desk. "I'll explain the poem in a minute."

"Yes, Sister Bunkai," replied Aki, who had just entered the Ryokuin'an study.

Lowering herself onto the cushion at her desk, Aki began examining the poem that Bunkai had placed there for her to copy. She picked up the water dropper—a tiny ceramic vessel shaped like a frog—and began preparing her ink. She tilted the frog so that several drops of water fell from its open mouth onto the sloping surface of the rectangular slab of her ink-stone. The water ran down and formed a small pool in the recess at the lower part of the stone. Aki took an ink stick and, with repeated circular motions, rubbed one of its short ends through the water across the smooth black surface of the stone, creating dark glistening pigment. She sniffed, catching the smoky and woody scents that had been added to the mix of soot and glue as the ink stick was being manufactured.

Once Aki had a puddle of ink to work with, she took a sheet of paper and placed it next to the poem. She picked up a writing brush, dipped the tip into her ink and began to write.

As Aki copied the vertical lines, silence enveloped the room. After an hour, though, she became restless. With a soft cough, she caught her teacher's attention and said, "Sister Bunkai, I heard something very strange. I was hoping you might explain what it means."

"What did you hear, Aki?"

"Well, the other day I was heading into town—"

"And?"

"And I was passing by the entrance to the new temple grounds, just beyond the Otowa River." As Aki went on, she began babbling in a nervous, roundabout manner. "You know, Sister Bunkai, it's that place you told me about, where an imperial abbot is building a temple. It's been busy over there lately. Lots of workers have been showing up. When do you think the gardens will be done? Do you think I'll catch a glimpse of the abbot who's building the temple?"

Tucking her chin, Bunkai peered at her student. "What *is* your question, Aki?"

Aki tugged at the sleeves of her gray robe, and then, looking directly at her teacher, she stated, "There were two gentlemen at the entrance to the new temple."

Bunkai frowned, saying, "There were?"

"Uh, huh." Aki struggled to speak in an even tone, but she could hear the agitation in her own voice. "They didn't know I was nearby. But I wasn't eavesdropping."

"You heard something, Aki?"

"I did." Aki paused before plunging ahead. "One of the gentlemen said the retired emperor was forced to marry the shōgun's daughter."

Aki stopped to check her teacher's expression. Unable to read Bunkai's reaction, she went on. "I think that gentleman might have been a member of the emperor's court."

"What else?"

"One of the gentlemen claimed there was a fire at the palace blamed on a couple girls. He said the emperor can't train with a sword. And the emperor might be abducted. The other man—I think he was a priest—agreed with him."

Coming to an abrupt halt, Aki averted her gaze from the nun. She stared at dust motes hovering in the air, illuminated by a shaft of light entering the room through a long, narrow gap between the doors to the garden. She squirmed. She wondered how Bunkai was reacting. She wanted to look over at her teacher, but she didn't have the nerve. Her unease grew.

Finally, Bunkai responded. While running one hand across her lap to straighten the wrinkles in her robe, she answered coolly, saying, "I don't really know, Aki. That conversation seems quite unusual."

Aki presumed Bunkai would answer her question. However, Bunkai remained quiet. Frowning, the nun sat quietly, staring out into the garden.

"I didn't mean to eavesdrop, Sister Bunkai. I'm sorry."

"No need to apologize, Aki. Tell me, when did this happen?"

"Three days ago. Early in the morning. You know, I often pass by that spot on my way into town."

"Do you remember anything else?"

"Well, the gentlemen were also talking about the troubles facing the rōnin. They said the rōnin warriors have no master, and they're miserable. That's all I remember, Sister Bunkai."

"Aki, did the two men refer to each other by name?"

"No." Aki paused for a moment and asked, "What were they talking about anyway?"

"I can't explain it, Aki. But let me know if you remember hearing their names," Bunkai added. The study became still as Bunkai stared at her student. Then the nun rose up from her desk, saying, "I need to end your lesson early, Aki."

"But Sister Bunkai, I only finished six copies."

"That's alright. It's enough for today. I'll be waiting for you first thing in the morning, Aki. Understood?"

There was nothing for Aki to do but agree and follow the nun's instructions. As she put her writing utensils away, Bunkai went to the door and waited. Once Aki had cleared off her desk, she rose up and left the room, staring mutely at her feet as Bunkai closed the door behind her.

Walking away from the Ryokuin'an, Aki wondered what to think. Bunkai is rarely this curt, she said to herself. Why did she dismiss me so early? Did she decide I'm too nosey? I thought my inquisitiveness was a good thing.

✼ ✼ ✼

Trudging up the last leg of the steep forest trail toward home, Aki was greeted by waving fronds of ferns and butterflies that flittered above velvety mounds of jade colored moss. But Aki hardly noticed any of that.

Reaching her gate, Aki spotted her mother in the yard. Natsu had stayed home for the day and was retrieving bedding from a line in the yard, where it had been airing out. Grasping two woven coverlets, Natsu stopped with a look of concern. "Aki, was there a problem at the convent? You're home early."

"No. No problem. Sister Bunkai is just busy."

"There's something on the stove for you," Natsu remarked, heading toward the hut. Inside, she laid the bedding on the raised plank flooring before going to the stove and dishing up a bowl of rice porridge.

Aki followed her mother into the kitchen.

Handing the bowl to her daughter, Natsu remarked, "I need to go speak with the headman."

"Alright," Aki mumbled.

"I shouldn't be gone more than an hour."

Aki sat to eat the porridge as her mother left. Before long, she was standing and putting her empty bowl on the counter. Then, leaving to do chores, she grabbed her firewood basket and climbed up one of the slopes a short distance from her hut. She gathered sticks and twigs, cut them into segments, piled them into her basket and returned home. In the yard, she bound together three bundles of kindling for her morning deliveries. Then, she began winding hemp cord, perched on a tree stump.

At this point, Natsu returned and joined her daughter. Natsu took a seat on a stool, and the two began discussing the weather.

Aki noticed that her mother seemed quite calm. Each of Natsu's slender eyebrows formed a gentle curve. Her small mouth, which sat low on her face, was relaxed, her lower lip smooth and full. When Natsu glanced up from her winding, Aki said, "May I ask you a question, mother?"

Natsu's eyes darted to meet her daughter's as she remarked, "Teinei na kotoba? You're using polite language again, Aki."

"Was I?"

"Yes, you were. I get suspicious when you speak that way. I'm not Sister Bunkai. I'm your mom. No need to speak so formally. What's your question?"

Aki nodded and plunged in. "Mom, how'd the rōnin end up with no warrior lord to serve?"

"You don't know, Aki? Well, I suppose I've avoided telling you about that sort of thing." Natsu sighed and went on to explain. "There are many reasons rōnin might have no lord. Their lord might have lost his lands in war or from government decree."

"And no one helps them find another lord to serve?"

"It doesn't work that way. It's complicated."

"Mom, do *you* know any rōnin?"

"Well, some of the men I meet when I'm out selling flowers are rōnin," answered Natsu. She reached up and tucked a dangling lock of hair behind one ear.

Aki grew quiet, considering her mother's response.

"Aki, I need to leave for a while this evening. I might be gone for several hours."

"Why?"

"The headman ordered the village women to take turns watching the fields."

"Why's that?"

"To chase off the animals coming out of the forest after sunset. They've been eating the crops. We also have to keep track of water in the irrigation channels. If there's any blockage, we need to clear it out."

"Why didn't the headman say I should join the night watch?"

Natsu shrugged, saying, "Maybe next year."

"Why not now?"

Natsu threw up her hands. "Aki! Stop pestering me with questions."

Aki pressed her lips together.

"The headman will probably be calling on me regularly for night duty through the rest of the summer. After I leave, you should bolt the door behind me and only open it again when you hear my voice, but no one else's. There's no reason to worry, though." Natsu cast a questioning glance at Aki.

"Alright, mom." Aki wondered why she hadn't been included in the night watch. After a short silence, she asked, "Mom, was the emperor told to marry the shōgun's daughter?"

"What?"

"Did the shōgun force the emperor to marry his daughter?"

"I wouldn't say that—" Natsu hesitated. "But you heard one of those two gentlemen say something like that. Didn't you, Aki?"

"Uh, huh. Which emperor were they talking about, mom?"

"I suppose it was retired Emperor GoMizunoo."

"The father of the Enshōji abbess?"

"Yes. He had an arranged marriage. Most people do."

"I see," Aki mumbled. "But you and dad didn't have an arranged marriage."

"Right. What I *should* say is that most people of high rank do," Natsu corrected herself.

"So—" Aki hesitated. "Who were those two gentlemen I overheard?"

"I don't know," answered Natsu before growing quiet. A moment passed, and then she stood to start dinner.

PART 2

BACKGROUND: THE RŌNIN PLIGHT

PATIENT READER, BY NOW YOU UNDERSTAND WHAT SERIOUS problems rōnin faced in 1654. Many were sons and grandsons of former samurai, well educated and steeped in a warrior ethos. Although their ancestors had been respected warrior retainers with legitimate legal standing as men of the sword, rōnin were not. When their ancestors were vanquished in battle or otherwise stripped of their titles and lands, they forfeited their warrior status.

To grasp the extent of difficulties rōnin faced, we go back to 1615 when, following a monumental battle, lords fighting for the Toyotomi experienced a crushing defeat at the hands of the Tokugawa. Then, lords who had supported the young Toyotomi heir were forced to release their retainers. As a result, thousands of warriors became lowly rōnin. And from that point forward, the ranks of rōnin expanded.

When the second and third Tokugawa shōguns continued with land confiscation and retainer dispossession, rōnin numbers grew larger still. The shōguns forbad lords from hiring rōnin without express permission from a previous lord, and, of course, if the former lord had died, that was impossible. Samurai already serving the shōgun were allowed to pass their retainership on to sons, but eventually there was little demand for the expertise of unemployed warriors.

Unable to make a living as samurai, rōnin had few options, especially after the Tokugawa made it illegal for people to change their social status. Masterless warriors, who once could've become artisans or a merchants, were no longer allowed take up a new profession. Although some adventurous rōnin managed to travel abroad to find work, they soon found themselves locked out and lonely as Edo authorities banned them from returning to Japan and forbad others from going abroad. For the rōnin, then, pacification of the realm by Tokugawa shōguns meant peace by coercion.

Yet, despite an unflagging determination to dominate the land, the shōgun could not govern as an out-and-out tyrant, nor did the rōnin roll over and disappear. Few events prove this more clearly than the rōnin insurrections that broke out soon after the death of the third Tokugawa shōgun. At this point, many of the hundreds of thousands of rōnin in the land—those rash enough and angry enough to revolt—rose up against the Tokugawa.

"Good. All's quiet," mumbled Deputy Inspector Tanaka to himself.

A few minutes earlier, Tanaka had said goodbye to his two agents, The Crab and The Wolf, and had embarked on the solitary part of his morning patrol. He was now approaching the Nijō estate north of the imperial palace. When he reached a point where tall perimeter walls were all he could see stretching ahead of him at both sides of the road, Tanaka came to a halt, tilted his head back and smelled the air. A breeze carried the fragrance of freshly cut Japanese cypress, which had been used to construct many of the fine aristocratic residences in this district. It was a fresh, calming scent.

Tanaka knew that the white-washed, earthen wall to his left bordered the Nijō estate at the north. As he followed the wall, his eyes swept up and down, back and forth. Nothing seemed unusual. At the next intersection of roadways, he turned left and continued on, now hugging the western wall. Nothing worrisome here, he decided. He made another left and headed toward the main entrance of the estate, the front gate at the center of its southern wall.

As he got closer to the front entrance, Tanaka began picking up voices from behind the Nijō gate. He hung back and watched as the gate opened and a palanquin emerged, covered in gold-on-black lacquered designs. Large enough to accommodate one person, the palanquin was suspended from a single long pole. A porter at the front had hoisted one end of the pole and placed it over his right shoulder, as a porter at the back lifted up the other end to carry on his own shoulder.

A group of ladies followed the palanquin. Each wore a gauze scarf draped over a wide brimmed hat to obscure her face. As the group passed by the deputy inspector, he glanced down at the women's fine footwear. Their sandals had been expertly crafted with leather soles and bamboo skin. Two male escorts bearing swords brought up the rear.

When the parade of ladies had moved off, another gorgeous palanquin emerged from the main gate of the Nijō estate. Emblazoned on its roof was a distinctive golden design of floral sprays, the Nijō family crest. The deputy inspector recognized it as the regent's vehicle, and he recalled having seen it often outside the palace and at certain aristocratic residences. Another pair of armed guards trailed behind the regent.

Once they had passed, Tanaka started up again and made his way toward the Nijō gate.

The gate guard was there, standing erect as usual. The man called out, "Good day, Deputy Inspector Tanaka. How are your rounds this morning?"

"All's well, thank you." Tanaka dipped his head. "I see that the regent and ladies of the household have departed."

"Yes, sir. Hai! They're attending ceremonies for an ancestor of the Nijō family."

"I see. No problem on the estate, then?"

"No, sir. I checked the grounds before the master and mistress left for the temple. I found nothing out of the ordinary."

"That's good to hear. I'll be on my way, then."

"Yes, sir. Take care in the heat, sir."

"You, too," the deputy inspector replied before turning and resuming his route. He made his way westward toward the next mansion. After circumambulating and scrutinizing the exterior of the neighboring estate, Tanaka concluded that all was in order there. Retracing his steps, he returned to the spot near the Nijō gate.

That's when the deputy inspector noticed something unusual. From a half block away, Tanaka could see that the wooden gate at the front of the Nijō compound was half ajar. No one seemed to be standing watch.

An alarm sounded in the deputy inspector's head. The Nijō guard has never been this careless before, Tanaka said to himself. He removed the dagger from under his wide sash and cautiously approached the gate.

Within seconds, the deputy inspector was pushing the gate open and peering in. What he saw was unexpected. The guard Tanaka had just been speaking with was slumped over on the flagstone. The deputy inspector crouched down to examine him, seeing a deep red welt around the guard's neck. Tanaka realized immediately the guard was dead. He'd been strangled.

The deputy inspector glanced around warily, but the estate was quiet. As he rose up, he caught sight of an elderly man cowering in the shadows at one side of the residence.

"You there!" called out the deputy inspector.

A quavering voice responded. "Yes, sir."

"I am Deputy Inspector Tanaka Taisuke. Are you a servant here?"

The man stepped forward, trembling. "Yes, sir. I am the butler on the Nijō estate."

"What happened? Did you see anything?"

"I did, sir. It was Shining Blade. He snuck into the master's private study and stole his letters," the butler answered with a grimace. "Then he killed the gateman and ran off."

Tanaka nodded slowly, scanning the grounds. "He left the premises?"

"Yes, sir. He's gone."

"Take me to the study of the Nijō regent," commanded Tanaka.

Complying, the butler led Tanaka to the steps at the entrance of the residence and slipped out of his geta clogs as Tanaka removed his straw sandals. The butler ushered the deputy inspector up a short flight of stairs, across the threshold, down a hallway with finely polished flooring, past a series of chambers and across a veranda that extended to the study.

The door of the study stood open, revealing a room in disarray. A carved wooden desk lay overturned on its side. Scrolls were thrown about with writing brushes and papers strewn across the floor. The deputy inspector noticed that one of the doors opposite him was standing open. He crossed the room and peered into the garden.

Tanaka stepped outside and surveyed the garden. Leaving the veranda, he went to search for anything the intruder might have left behind. He bent down on one of the flat stepping stones, pushing aside bunches of tall grass to get a closer look. Seeing nothing unusual, the deputy inspector stepped over a patch of moss and peered beneath a cluster of painted ferns, their bluish-green fronds touched with silvery edges. Met only by the damp, musty smell of the soil's organic elements, Tanaka continued searching.

At last, Tanaka spotted something that didn't belong, an object coiled up and tossed onto the ground. It lay beyond a row of hedges next to the wall at the west side of the estate. As the deputy inspector drew near, he recognized it as a rope ladder. A few feet away lay a grappling hook. Tanaka reached down and picked up the hook, realizing it had once been attached to the rope ladder.

Walking back across the garden, Tanaka reconstructed mentally what must have happened. The thief had waited, knowing somehow that members of the Nijō family planned to leave that morning. Then, once the family had departed, the thief used the rope ladder to scale the Nijō garden wall and enter the quiet compound.

The deputy inspector reviewed his earlier examination of the west exterior wall of the Nijō estate and quickly came to another realization. "The robber arrived just after me!" Tanaka said under his breath. The intruder's entry onto the estate must have happened immediately after I left the front gate. The criminal must have acted swiftly, but the grappling hook became detached from the rope as he was using it. So, he tossed it aside, Tanaka concluded.

Wait! Was he following me? Tanaka wondered. Was he waiting for me to walk away from the estate? Does he know my regular rounds? Shaking his head, Tanaka brushed off the sense of someone watching him.

Climbing the stairway to the veranda, Tanaka considered what the thief had been after. Clearly, the fellow wanted something specific. And he knew where to find it—in the master's study. But the item the thief grabbed wasn't a valuable painting of a Buddhist deity or a rare sample of imperial handwriting. It was a box of letters.

Tanaka turned to the butler standing nearby and quizzed him. "You're certain? The thief stole a box of letters? That's all?"

The butler drew back, clearly intimidated. He answered timidly, "I believe so, sir. I saw him near the front gate as he was leaving. He was carrying a single item, the box of letters."

I need to change my tone, Tanaka cautioned himself as he bit the inside of his cheek. I don't want this butler becoming reticent. He's likely the only person who witnessed the murder first-hand.

"Would you be able to describe how the thief murdered the gateman?" the deputy inspector queried, his voice now calmer.

The butler nodded. "The thief approached the gate attendant from behind. Then he quietly set down the box of letters to strangle the man. I'm so sorry I couldn't stop him, sir." Looking wretched, the butler dropped his head and, hugging himself, rubbed his upper arms.

"And could you describe the thief?" asked Tanaka.

"Yes, sir. He was young, maybe twenty years old. And rather tall."

"What was he wearing?"

"He had on black leggings and a dark green jacket. Can you imagine, sir? Such warm clothing on a day like this?"

Surprised, Tanaka took a step back. Shaking his head, he asked himself, was it that rōnin swordsman from the other morning, the one performing on the empty lot near the bridge?

Tanaka recalled the scene several days earlier, when he had been standing in the shade at a spot near the confluence of the Takano and Kamo Rivers. He and his two agents had been discussing the sword-wielding performance of a tall, young rōnin wearing dark leggings and a jacket with pine needle design.

"Tell me," Tanaka addressed the butler again. "Was there a design on the thief's jacket?"

"Yes, sir. It had pine needles."

Tanaka was floored, realizing that the thief and the sword performer might be one and the same. Did he follow me on my patrol that day? Tanaka asked himself. Did he leave the empty lot right after I was watching him!

"Why'd he do it, sir?" the butler lamented. "Why'd he go and kill an innocent guard? Could a box of letters be so important?"

Shaking his head, the deputy inspector took a deep breath. Then he remarked, "A few minutes ago you identified the thief as Shining Blade. What makes you think it was him?"

"Well, sir, I've been told Shining Blade is quite lanky. And he has a prominent scar at the left side of his face. Our thief was tall and lean, and he had a jagged mark running down his left temple."

"I see," Tanaka replied.

"Sir, could I make a request of you? Could you please speak with my master, Lord Nijō? I know he'll be distressed by news of the gateman's death. Please, sir, I implore you— tell his lordship I couldn't have saved the gateman. It just wasn't possible."

"Of course. I'll explain things to the regent."

The butler wiped sweat from his forehead and bowed.

Tanaka went on. "Your observations will be of great value to the Second Street magistrate. He will want to hear your testimony. And Magistrate Gomi will convey the information to the Kyoto governor. Governor Itakura will decide the matter."

"Thank you, sir!" The butler bowed, bending forward from the waist.

Turning his attention back to the crime scene, Tanaka inquired, "Can someone run to the local police box to inform authorities of this incident?"

Nodding, the butler called out, and a cowering, young kitchen maid emerged from the far side of the residence.

"Go to the police," Tanaka ordered. "Report a crime. Tell them a man's been murdered. I need them to bring a cart."

The girl bowed, jumped and ran off through the gate. The butler went inside to wait in the mansion, while Tanaka continued outside, searching the grounds.

Some time later, four policemen arrived, two pushing a narrow flatbed on wheels. The deputy inspector introduced himself to them, before explaining the situation and ordering them to remove the body of the gateman. He watched them lift the lifeless body onto the cart.

Once they were gone, Tanaka turned to the butler, saying, "Inform Lord Nijō that I will compose a report about what I encountered here. I will return at his convenience to answer any questions."

"Yes, sir." The butler bowed deeply.

With that, Tanaka set off for his study. He needed to write a report concerning the incident. He was confident that the news would quickly be passed up the chain of command and reach his boss's boss. The deputy inspector felt certain that the Kyoto governor would hear about it by the end of the day. Tanaka wanted his report to accurately convey what he had encountered at the regent's mansion.

"Aki, we need to talk," said Bunkai.

Aki lifted her writing brush and looked up questioningly.

An hour earlier, Aki had arrived at the Ryokuin'an study, greeted her teacher and taken a seat to study the scroll laid out for her by the nun. The scroll contained columns of names written in formal script. After preparing her ink in silence, Aki had begun her transcription.

"I was thinking—" Bunkai hesitated.

"About what?" Aki interjected. "The things I overheard? Sister Bunkai, I regret listening in on a private conversation. I should've known it was wrong."

"No. That's not it, Aki. You were right to inform me."

Aki felt a bit confused.

The nun adjusted her position to sit even straighter than usual. "There's something I must ask of you, Aki."

Aki focused on her teacher.

"Would you help us? It's not for my sake, Aki. It's for the imperial family."

Eyes wide, Aki asked, "You want me to help the imperial family?"

"Yes. You could help them greatly."

Aki squared her shoulders. "I'll do whatever I can. What is it you want me to do, Sister Bunkai?"

"I need you to carry secret letters for Abbess Bunchi."

"That's all?"

"Yes. You should continue delivering the firewood, like you're doing already. But I need you to stop by here every morning on your way into town so I can insert a letter into each of your three kindling bundles."

"Alright." Aki nodded.

"And at each spot where you drop off firewood, I need you to look for a letter meant for Abbess Bunchi. When the master or the abbot or abbess at one of your delivery locations has a letter for Abbess Bunchi, they'll place it in a ceramic pot with a blue lid sitting near their kitchen entrance. If you find a letter, you'll need to take it and hide it up your sleeve. There's plenty of room for letters there. The letters shouldn't drop out. If there's no letter in the ceramic pot, you simply move on. The letters are secret, so they won't be addressed to the reverend mother, but after you bring them back to me, I'll pass them on to her."

"What's in the letters, Sister Bunkai?"

"Nothing that concerns you, Aki."

"Oh!" Aki pulled her chin back momentarily, but then her face relaxed and she said, "That sounds easy enough."

"I hope so. This won't require any change to your current schedule, Aki, other than stopping by here in the morning and again in the afternoon. It's simply a matter of continuing your regular deliveries and dropping off the letters and bringing others back to me."

"I'll do it!"

"You'll need to keep quiet about the letters. And *don't* try to read them."

"Of course not."

"Good. We will start tomorrow," the nun said, sounding relieved. "Stop by here before you leave for town."

"Yes, Sister Bunkai."

"Good. Now that's settled, we should get back to work."

Aki nodded and resumed her transcription.

An hour later, Bunkai spoke again, now bringing up a new subject. "Aki, I suspect you might like to catch a glimpse of one of the abbess's relatives."

"Sure! Which one?"

"The Manshuin abbot, Reverend Ryōshō. He's the head priest of the new temple going up near here."

"Manshuin? The temple on the other side of the river?"

"That's right. The abbot is overseeing work at the construction site. He'll be stopping here now and then."

"What's he like, Sister Bunkai?"

"Well, he's dedicated and sincere."

"Is he older than the Enshōji abbess?"

"No. He's four years younger than her. Ryōshō's father was the uncle of the abbess's father."

"Then—" Aki hesitated. "The Manshuin abbot is her cousin. Right?"

"Something like that. Abbot Ryōshō is her father's cousin once removed."

"Uh, huh," Aki nodded, her eyes wide.

Bunkai smiled and, lifting one eyebrow, she challenged her student, saying, "Try to memorize the names in that genealogy, Aki."

"Alright," replied Aki confidently.

*　　*　　*

"Pickles!" Aki said under her breath, having caught a whiff of something familiar.

It was early afternoon, and Aki was alone, approaching the Yamabana Market. Before leaving Enshōji, she had promised Sister Bunkai she would go to the market and pick up provisions for the convent.

No mistaking that smell. So strong and pungent, Aki thought. She turned and spotted three large bowls sitting under the awning of a new stall at her right. The bowls were filled with pickled white radish preserved in fermented soybean paste. As a child, Aki had hated the smell of those pickles, but when she learned that Sister Bunkai loved them, her reaction changed. Now she appreciated the bold flavor of the radishes smothered in the sweet red and brown marinade.

Aki picked up her pace. She passed by rows of counters and headed for a specific vegetable stall, the one operated by a wizened and wiry-haired woman named Mari. Everyone who frequented the market knew Mari. Some, intimidated by Mari's sharp tongue, headed in the opposite direction when they caught a glimpse of her. Not Aki, though. Even though Aki cringed when she heard Mari snapping at a perplexed customer, she always looked forward to speaking with the sassy stall keeper. And Mari had reciprocated, encouraging Aki to call her Granny Mari.

Before even uttering a hello, Mari groaned. "Ugh! Can you believe this muggy weather?"

Aki was about to reply when Mari cut her off, complaining, "Everything's limp and damp."

Aki nodded her agreement.

"Standing here all day, my clothes just stick to my sweaty back."

"I know," Aki replied. "It's so humid my sandals slip around when I'm gathering twigs for my firewood bundles."

"That's not good." Mari scowled. "And this hair of mine! It frizzes up and, when I bend forward to wait on customers, it sticks to my forehead."

Aki glanced at Mari's unruly gray curls.

"The little bit of hair I got! He, he!" Mari added with a cackle. "Say, Little Aki. Did you hear? That rōnin thief was seen near here."

"Shining Blade?"

"Yup. That's what they call him."

"When?"

"Yesterday, late afternoon," Mari answered. "A couple weeks ago, he was downtown stealing swords. Now he's in our neck of the woods."

"That's scary!"

"Yup. Say, what are you here for, Little Aki?"

"The Enshōji kitchen needs some things—salt, tea, dried kelp and cooking oil."

"Let me get those ready for you," Mari remarked, grabbing several sheets of the paper sitting at the side of her counter.

Meanwhile, Aki surveyed the market. She wondered whether the thief might be nearby. She examined the customers, but no one seemed particularly dangerous.

Mari started measuring tea and piling it into a mound on one of her medium-size sheets of paper. She folded the paper into a neat, secure packet. Next she did the same with salt and then dried kelp. After that, she grabbed a small jar with a stopper from the shelf behind her. Finally, she pulled out a fabric square and placed everything in the middle of it before bringing the four corners together and tying them in a knot at the top, creating a tidy bundle. She handed the bundle to Aki, saying, "There you are, young miss."

"Thank you, Granny Mari. See you next time."

"Yup. Now off you go. Don't slip and slide on the forest path."

"I won't." Aki smiled at the stall keeper. Holding the package by its sturdy knot, she started off for the convent kitchen.

KURŌBEI AND GORŌ

"WE'RE HERE," CALLED OUT A MAN IN INDIGO GARMENTS, A swordsman hired by Ishida Kurōbei to instruct recruits.

Trailing behind the instructor was an older, broad-shouldered man. The two had just arrived at an old barn at the end of a lonely path on the outskirts of eastern Kyoto, and now they were stepping single file over the threshold.

The older man paused and looked around the large, shadowy interior. Spotting a lone figure in the middle of the barn, he called out, "Hello, Master Kurōbei!"

Kurōbei turned to face the new arrivals. He immediately recognized the older one as Shimada Gorō, a rōnin who had served his now deceased father.

"Ah, Mister Shimada! It's been a while," Kurōbei responded cordially. He approached and grabbed Gorō robustly by the shoulders, holding him firmly at an arm's length and fixing his eyes on the man.

"Yes, it has been a while. Your man was waiting for me where you said he'd be." Gorō gestured toward the instructor in blue making his way across the barn toward two others. The three instructors, easily differentiated by the color of their garments, lowered themselves to sit on their haunches.

"You seem little changed, Mister Shimada. Except your hair."

Gorō reached up to smooth down a stray gray hair that had worked its way free from the black silk cord, holding together the tail at the back of his neck. He nodded, saying, "I'm glad to see you looking well, young master. And free!"

"Indeed," Kurōbei responded resolutely. "I plan to stay that way. Tell me, how long have you been in Kyoto?"

"About two months."

"And you came here from Edo?"

"That's right," Gorō nodded. Looking around the barn, he added, "You set up this training center quickly. Congratulations."

Kurōbei lifted his chin and, looking satisfied, answered, "There's work to do here."

"You're gathering instructors and recruits?"

"Yes. Men have started coming from all over to train here."

"They're mostly rōnin?"

"They *all* are," answered Kurōbei, nodding with a bit of a smile. "Let me show you around, Mister Shimada. First, though, I'll introduce you to my instructors."

Kurōbei ushered Gorō across the barn toward the three men, each of whom rose up to take a formal stance. As Kurōbei gave their names and their backgrounds, they bowed. Then it was Gorō's turn to lower his head as Kurōbei told the instructors about him.

Continuing the tour, Kurōbei moved to a tall, wide stand near the closest wall, where row after row of practice blades had been arranged horizontally. Gesturing toward the training weapons, which were a bit longer than swords made of steel, Kurōbei remarked, "All of these are made of the best hardwoods."

Gorō dipped his head and Kurōbei moved on, describing other features of the training facility. Finally, Kurōbei pointed toward several cushions set beside a short table near the doorway and said, "Have a seat, Mister Shimada."

As Gorō went to sit at the table, Kurōbei headed to the opposite corner of the barn. Opening a wicker basket, he pulled out a saké gourd and two small cups. He carried the gourd and cups to the table, saying, "Let's have a drink, Mister Shimada."

Kurōbei took a seat and poured saké for each of them. They lifted their cups, calling out "Kanpai," and quickly downed their drinks.

"You say you've only been in the old capital for two months, Mister Shimada, but that's longer than me," Kurōbei stated. "What can you tell me about the Gion Festival?"

"Well, it's Kyoto's biggest summer festival, somewhat like the one they held in that town near us in Tanba. Kyoto residents gather for a procession of floats to launch the festival." Gorō stopped for a moment before adding, "That's a little over a week from now."

Becoming quiet, Kurōbei rubbed his chin in thought.

Gorō observed the younger man watchfully for several minutes. Then he cleared his throat and inquired, "Young master, are you teaching your recruits the code of the samurai?"

"What?" asked Kurōbei, emerging from his deliberations.

"Are you teaching your recruits the principles of honor that your father upheld?" Gorō clarified.

Pulling back his chin, Kurōbei replied, "My father?"

"Yes. Master Masanori was a respected warrior, as was his grandfather."

"That drivel about principles isn't for me," Kurōbei responded sharply. "My father was a great man, but what happened back in Tanba was tragic. And now it's ancient history."

Gorō twisted his lips to one side for a moment before remarking, "Your father's legacy lives on, Kurōbei."

Clearly irritated, Kurōbei replied, "Before I was born, the Ishida served the leader of Fukuchiyama domain in Tanba for two generations. But we were dispossessed. Now we're just impoverished rōnin."

"Even impoverished rōnin can maintain their dignity by honorable action."

Kurōbei's angry retort was immediate. "No! That's not so! The only way for us to maintain our dignity is to fight."

"Now, Kurōbei! I wouldn't say that—"

Interrupting, Kurōbei snarled, "Which side are you on, Mister Shimada?"

"Young master, you know I respected your father greatly," Gorō replied in a conciliatory tone.

Veins having risen on his forehead, Kurōbei blurted out, "Either you fight *with* me or against me, Shimada!"

Gorō paused. "As you know, young master, I promised your father I would protect you with my life."

"And therefore?"

"I won't break my promise to your father."

"I take that to mean you'll fight with me," Kurōbei declared, standing and gesturing toward the barn door, not giving Gorō a chance to qualify his position any further. He added, "Let's go find something to eat."

"SISTER BUNKAI, DO YOU MIND IF I TELL MY MOTHER I'M DELIVering secret letters for the abbess?" asked Aki.

It was early on a muggy morning, and Aki had returned to the Ryokuin'an for a lesson. She had already started her transcription when she remembered what she'd wanted to ask the nun.

"Aki, that's not a good idea," Bunkai replied.

"But she's bound to find out that I'm stopping by here every morning on my way into town. What should I tell her?"

"Well, I'm afraid you're right," Bunkai paused. "Alright. But Mistress Natsu must promise to keep the matter secret. And tell no one else."

"Of course," Aki answered, picking up her brush again. She breathed in deeply, catching the sooty, earthy scent rising up from her inkstone, and resumed her copying.

After another hour had passed, she glanced at the nun, set her brush down and cleared her throat. Hoping to learn more about a topic that had fascinated her for days now, she said, "Sister Bunkai, you were telling me about a rōnin revolt in Edo. When did that happen?"

"You're referring to the Edo Insurrection of 1651?"

"I guess so."

"Your mother didn't tell you about it, Aki?"

"No," Aki replied, shaking her head. She didn't want to admit that her mother had explained a few things about the insurrection, but then refused to answer any of her questions. Aki asked, "Who was involved?"

"There were two leaders. One was Yui Shōsetsu—"

Aki repeated the name, "Yui Shōsetsu." She was now leaning forward with her elbows on her desk and her chin resting in one palm.

Bunkai continued. "Shōsetsu was born in Sunpu to a talented fabric dyer. He even started his own business manufacturing weapons and armor, not far from Edo. I heard he was successful and that people praised him for being industrious and enterprising. All the while, however, Shōsetsu was recruiting men to his cause."

"So, Shōsetsu was sneaking around planning to cause trouble?"

"Well, I wouldn't say *that*, Aki. Shōsetsu channeled the frustrations of many rōnin. The ruling authorities in Edo had issued numerous laws and decrees in their attempt to curtail rōnin activities."

"I see."

"Shōsetsu invited men from former samurai families to join him. Most of those men had been dispossessed by their lord. Shōsetsu taught them how to improve their fighting skills, and he encouraged them to study military history."

"I see," Aki repeated, a bit surprised at the amount of information her teacher was providing. Usually, Bunkai only offered a few details. Wanting to learn more, Aki asked, "Was Shōsetsu the main leader of the Edo rōnin uprising?"

"Yes. But Marubashi Chūya played an important role, too. If it hadn't been for Chūya, the uprising might have succeeded." Bunkai shot her student an uncertain glance before adding, "Let's forget about all that and resume our work. Shall we, Aki?"

"No, wait! Are you saying that the Tokugawa authorities discovered the rōnin plan?"

Bunkai nodded. "Chūya was executed, and Shōsetsu took his own life. It was terrible."

Aki sat wide-eyed, hoping Bunkai would tell her more. However, the nun had finished her account and had turned her attention back to a document on her desk.

Aki dropped her shoulders with a sigh, picked up her brush and resumed her copying.

The two women worked quietly for another long stretch. Then, a loud clang rang out from the courtyard. Startled, Aki felt herself jump.

"Sounds like someone dropped a pail in the courtyard," Bunkai remarked. "Nothing serious, I'm sure."

"Uh, huh," Aki mumbled. Lowering her eyes again, she was about to resume her transcription, when she glanced back up and asked, "Weren't the rōnin worried their plot would be discovered by the shōgun's men?"

Surprised, the nun frowned, but then she shrugged and answered. "The rōnin knew the shōgun's advisors were distracted. They meant to strike at a vulnerable time for the central government."

"Why was that a vulnerable time, Sister Bunkai?"

"You must know, Aki, that the third shōgun died three years ago in June."

Aki nodded. Then, cocking her head, she began wondering what the death of the third shōgun had to do with the insurrection.

Bunkai explained, "Soon after his death, the Edo rōnin began preparing their attack. They intended to strike in September. Even though the fourth shōgun had already been named, he was just a boy. With a such an inexperienced leader, things were precarious for the Tokugawa government."

"Oh, I see! Are things still precarious?" Aki asked. "Is the shōgun old enough now? Has he become a strong leader yet?"

"He has matured, but he still needs his advisors—the Edo Elders—to assist him. The question is, will the Elders continue the policy of seizing lands and dispossessing warriors who've lost their lord? Some say the rōnin's troubles are perpetuated by those Edo policies."

"I see," Aki repeated, more slowly now.

Once again, the room became quiet, and Aki returned to her work. Soon, however, she looked up and blurted out a question she'd been thinking about for days. Even she was surprised by her boldness in asking. "Would the emperor agree?"

Bunkai's eyes darted toward her student. "Agree to what, Aki?"

Embarrassed by her own impetuous question, Aki pressed her lips together for a moment. Then she rephrased her question. "What I meant to ask, Sister Bunkai, is—do you think the emperor knows that the rōnin want his help? And if they ask, would his majesty agree?"

"I am sure his majesty knows, Aki. I doubt he'd be able to agree."

"But—" Aki hesitated and, seeing the severe expression on her teacher's face, she picked up her brush, mumbling, "Never mind."

Another hour passed with Aki focusing on her transcription. When midday arrived, she heard Bunkai exhale. She looked up to see her teacher stretching her arms overhead.

"Shall we clear our desks?" suggested Bunkai.

Aki understood this as her cue to finish up and prepare to leave. She put her utensils back in their box and stacked her sheets of transcription on her desk in a neat formation.

"I'll be waiting for you first thing tomorrow, Aki."

"I'll be here."

When Bunkai stood to leave her study, Aki followed. The nun slid the shoji to the side, and the two women stepped through the doorway with Bunkai in the lead. They headed down the stairs and into the courtyard, where they said their goodbyes.

"STATE YOUR BUSINESS!" THE GUARD DEMANDED, CALLING OUT to the officer outside the main gate of Second Street Encampment.

"Deputy Inspector Tanaka Taisuke here. Summoned by Magistrate Gomi."

"Yes, sir," answered the guard as he signaled for his colleague to open the gate.

The previous evening, Tanaka had received orders to report early the following morning for a meeting with the Second Street magistrate, Gomi Toyonao. This was a first for Tanaka. Never before had he shown up alone for an appointment with Magistrate Gomi, who held a rank two rungs above his in the Kyoto hierarchy.

Tanaka wore a freshly cleaned uniform, consisting of an indigo jacket tucked into brown pants with wide pleats. A few minutes earlier, he had left his home nearby and had marched past Second Street Castle, headquarters of the Tokugawa shōgun in the old capital and the estate of the Kyoto governor. Continuing on toward the west, he had made his way to Second Street Encampment.

The guard opened the gate, bowed stiffly, turned and escorted Tanaka to Gomi's office. Arriving at the largest building on the compound, the guard slipped out of his footwear, ascended a short flight of stairs and proceeded down the wooden deck of a zigzagging veranda. Tanaka followed. With each step they took, the veranda boards squeaked as the nightingale floors announced their movements.

Once they had arrived at a quiet spot, the guard stopped to open a sliding door, revealing the interior of the magistrate's elegant office. Gomi was nowhere to be seen. A single cushion sat on the tatami mats at the middle of the room, across from a large desk. The guard gestured toward the cushion, indicating that the deputy inspector should take his place there.

As Tanaka entered the office, the guard informed him that the magistrate would arrive momentarily. Tanaka lowered himself onto the cushion. Maintaining the formalities of elite warrior society, the guard bowed once. Then he pivoted, closed the door and was gone.

Sitting perfectly erect, Tanaka positioned his palms flat on his thighs. Taking in the scent of new tatami—a fresh, slightly sweet and grassy smell—Tanaka began considering the written report he had submitted to Magistrate Gomi on the previous day. It concerned recent incidents involving masterless warriors. Did I leave anything out? Tanaka asked himself. Is that why the magistrate summoned me? Or does the magistrate have information to relate?

Tanaka heard footsteps. The door slid open, and the magistrate entered. His escort remained at attention on the veranda.

Tanaka bowed deeply, nearly touching his head to the tatami. He made out sounds of the escort closing the door and Gomi taking a seat at his desk.

Although his head was lowered, Tanaka knew quite well what the Second Street magistrate looked like. He'd seen Gomi numerous times in formal processions and at group audiences. Tanaka pictured the magistrate. He'll be wearing the requisite warrior's hairstyle with his pate recently shaved, Tanaka thought. He'll have his thick, gray mustache carefully trimmed. No doubt about it. Now, the deputy inspector recalled how Gomi's mouth slanted downward at one side and how creases under his chin extended to his collar.

Hearing Gomi clear his throat, Tanaka lifted his head and returned to his upright seated position. He kept his gaze fixed downward on the tatami, however. The deputy inspector was surprised to note, out the corner of his vision, that the magistrate was wearing formal garments—a kamishimo, consisting of a stiff sleeveless jacket with clan crests emblazoned on the chest and trailing, pleated trousers over a robe.

Gomi set his palms on his desktop and stated in a hoarse voice, "Deputy Inspector Tanaka, I've just come from a meeting with Governor Itakura. I need you to review with me what you know about recent criminal assaults in town."

"Yes, your excellency," responded Tanaka, who then launched into a concise recounting of incidents in Kyoto, concluding with a description of the three most brazen attacks. "Sir, nearly a month ago, there was a theft of two fine swords, accompanied by the killing of a shop clerk.

Not long after that a night-time attack at the estate of Katō Gosaemon resulted in the looting of the family storehouse and the death of two guards. A third egregious crime was the recent break-in at the estate of Regent Nijō, where a gate guard was strangled. All the thief took from the regent's mansion was a box of private letters."

Gomi nodded slowly, looking over Tanaka's shoulder and across the office. When he finally spoke again, he asked, "Do you have a suspect in mind for the three assaults, Tanaka?"

"Your excellency—" Tanaka paused. "I have reason to believe Ishida Kurōbei committed those crimes."

"Ishida Kurōbei?" the magistrate asked with a scowl.

"Yes, sir. He is the young rōnin criminal calling himself Shining Blade."

"Ah! Did Kurōbei act alone in each instance?" Gomi queried.

"Apparently, he did, sir."

"Tell me what you know about this lawless rōnin, Tanaka."

"Unfortunately, I know little about Ishida Kurōbei's background, sir. It seems, however, that he is fairly new to Kyoto."

"Hmm," mumbled Gomi as he began pulling on one earlobe. "No incidents this past week?"

"No, your excellency. None as serious. And none we suspect Ishida Kurōbei to have committed."

"Deputy Inspector Tanaka, is it possible this displaced warrior is done in Kyoto and that he has left town?"

"I suppose so, sir. But it seems unlikely."

"Why's that?"

"My agents have received reports of Shining Blade being seen around town in the past few days, sir."

Sitting back, Gomi resumed pulling his earlobe. Finally, he stated, "Tanaka, tell me what you know about the Edo Insurrection of 1651."

Surprised, Tanaka took a minute to collect what he'd heard about the rebellion three years earlier in the eastern capital of Edo. Then he began describing the plot hatched by two disgruntled rōnin, Yui Shōsetsu and Marubashi Chūya, explaining, "I was told that Chūya planned to use gunpowder to set fires inside Edo Castle. Then Shōsetsu was to rush in and kill the leading officials. Meanwhile, the flames would have spread beyond the Tokugawa governmental headquarters and destroyed many residences of elite lords in Edo."

Glancing up to see the magistrate gesturing for him to continue, the deputy inspector elaborated. He concluded by saying, "Their plot was discovered. Edo authorities quickly put an end to their intended revolt."

Gomi nodded quietly.

Tanaka wondered if there were significant details he had left out.

Clearing his throat again, Gomi stated, "Deputy inspector, did you know that the rōnin responsible for the Edo Insurrection of 1651 planned to attack representatives of the shōgun across the country?"

Tanaka's head jerked back. "Across the country, sir?"

Gomi watched Tanaka's reaction, as if to gauge how much the deputy inspector knew. Then he went on. "Yes.

They had colleagues in other provinces, even here in the old capital."

"I did not know that, sir."

Gomi shook his head, commenting, "I had presumed that your superior would inform you of these matters. Commissioner Wada told you very little, it seems."

Tanaka's eyebrows shot up when he heard Gomi openly criticize his boss. It was an awkward moment for him, but he needed to know more. He stumbled with uncertainty as he inquired, "May I ask, sir—were any rōnin arrested in Kyoto?"

"No. Unfortunately not, but the investigation is ongoing." Gomi paused, peering at Tanaka. "Deputy Inspector, you are not to discuss this with anyone outside the Office of the Kyoto Governor."

Tanaka was perplexed, but he nodded. "Understood, sir."

Looking directly into Tanaka's face, Gomi declared, "Those rōnin meant to gain access to the young sovereign."

"Emperor GoKōmyō!"

"Yes."

Tanaka sat back, grappling with the magistrate's revelation.

Gomi continued. "I am concerned this Ishida Kurōbei might be rallying displaced warriors in the larger region. And perhaps beyond. Do you have any reason to suspect that might be the case, Tanaka?"

"No, sir. I have heard nothing of the sort."

"We are entering a precarious time in the old capital, Tanaka."

"Sir?"

"It's festival season. The town will soon be overwhelmed with revelers," the magistrate declared. "The rōnin can easily hide amongst the townspeople."

Tanaka nodded, imagining the crowds that would come out for upcoming festivals.

Gomi let out a deep sigh and moved on to say, "On another matter, Tanaka, your superior will not be returning to Kyoto anytime soon. Not for another month, at least."

"I understand, sir." Tanaka gave a firm nod. "Sir, shall I send my reports on the Ishida Kurōbei case to Commissioner Wada?"

"No. Until the commissioner returns, submit your reports to me," answered Gomi. "And double the number of agents searching for Kurōbei."

"Yes, sir."

Gomi straightened his back, saying, "You may go now, deputy inspector."

"Yes, sir."

Tanaka bowed, stood and left the magistrate's office, heading back to his own study. He wasn't sure he was ready to take on so much new responsibility, but he had little to say in the matter. Something else bothered him, however. He couldn't help but question where his immediate superior, Commissioner Wada, had gone off to and why he had been away for so long.

PART 3

As you now realize, Careful Reader, Edo authorities confronted significant challenges in 1654, especially during the summer. In Kyoto, summertime meant festivals, and, with so many rōnin bent on protesting the shogunal presence in the old capital, that complicated the work of authorities.

One of the largest celebrations in Kyoto was the Gion Festival, held since the ninth century in the midsummer when hot, humid weather caused plagues. Thousands of festival goers emerged from their homes and workplaces, crowding together at streetside to watch lively song-and-dance entertainments and parades intended to appease the angry spirits that caused disease.

A highlight of the Gion Festival was the two-part float procession organized by townspeople belonging to block associations. Both parts included floats called mountains carried on men's shoulders, as well as larger floats with a tree or a branch projecting from the top. The biggest floats were tall and heavy, carrying singers, musicians and costumed children who stood in for the gods. These massive floats were pulled by men with ropes, following a charted route. The men came from sponsoring neighborhoods, which invested considerable time and money to ensure their float was the most magnificent of all.

The festival also featured a city tour of the numinous Gion deities, ensconced within sacred palanquins transported by volunteers. A team of male porters hoisted onto their shoulders one of the two long wooden beams that were attached under each sacred palanquin. Then they took off from Gion Shrine, moving through the streets and allowing the deities to mingle with people in town.

"IT'S ALL MEANT TO HONOR THE OX-HEADED HEAVENLY KING," explained Shimada Gorō.

"Ah!" replied Ishida Kurōbei, the younger of the two men sitting at a low table in the barn. Formerly a dilapidated, abandoned structure, the barn had been repurposed by Kurōbei as a training facility.

It was evening, and the barn interior was illuminated by several candles on tall metal stands. Gone were the instructors, who trained recruits with practice weapons during daylight hours on the dirt floor next to the table.

Kurōbei poured another round of saké and lifted his cup with a "Kanpai!" Once Gorō had mirrored his movements, they drank their wine. Then Kurōbei asked, "What more can you tell me about the festival?"

"Let's see—" Gorō paused before answering. "Kyoto residents implore the Heavenly king to intercede on behalf of the city and ensure a year free from pestilence."

Kurōbei, who had been pouring another round, stopped and snapped, "You told me that already! What about the Shinto floats?"

Gorō tossed back his drink and took a moment to recall what he'd heard. Then he continued. "People say that the floats are truly impressive, much bigger than any we've ever seen."

Peering at his older companion, Kurōbei listened attentively.

"The largest floats are two stories in height," Gorō explained. "Some have a temporary resting place for the gods."

Kurōbei filled the saké cups again and probed further. "Tell me about the float that comes at the end of the parade on the closing day."

"That's the Halberd float. It moves on wheels and carries entertainers."

"Yea, yea!" Kurōbei responded in irritation as he motioned with one hand, signaling Gorō to move on.

Not sure what Kurōbei was hoping to hear, Gorō added, "It's got a huge replica of a halberd at the top. The blade points toward the heavens. It supposedly has magical powers."

"Enough with the magic! Tell me, on the final day, where do the floats turn when they leave Fifth Street?"

Gorō shot Kurōbei a sideways glance, saying, "The floats turn left. Then they head north on Teramachi Avenue."

"Ah!" Kurōbei nodded. "How about the parade of palanquins?"

"Let's see—according to what I've heard, there are three sacred palanquins, gorgeously ornamented in gold leaf and crimson fabric. The palanquins get paraded around downtown. To lift the palanquin, the two groups of porters move in unison and hoist up one of the two beams attached at the bottom." With a huff, Gorō imitated the motions of the carriers, spiritedly lowering a shoulder and pretending to strain, lifting the palanquin.

"And?" asked Kurōbei, tapping the table with his thumb.

"The men carry the palanquins through the downtown."

"For how long?"

"For hours on end," Gorō answered. Stopping, he frowned and remarked, "Why not wait a short while and witness the festivities for yourself, young master?"

Responding with a quick shake of his head, Kurōbei went on to ask pointedly, "What route do the sacred palanquins take?"

"I heard the carriers leave Gion Shrine and head straight west on Fourth Street. They cross over the Kamo River and continue on for several more blocks."

Now Kurōbei sat back and folded his arms across his chest, listening to Gorō review the parade route of the sacred palanquins. When Gorō had revealed everything he knew, Kurōbei went silent, cocking his head to the left and staring down at his saké cup in thought.

AKI, NATSU AND THE GION FESTIVAL

"YOU'RE A SEXY ONE," SLURRED THE SCRAWNY, SHABBY MAN.

Having just left the shaded Yamabana Market, Aki had slowed for her eyes to adjust to the brightness of the street at midday. That's when the man had suddenly emerged from behind a row of wooden barrels, stepping right in front of her. Now coming to an abrupt halt, Aki pulled back her shoulders in surprise.

The man leered at Aki. He was wearing a tattered garment splattered with mud. Curling back his upper lip in a sneer, he croaked, "What's your name, sweetie?" His toothless mouth was close enough for Aki to smell his acrid breath.

Aki ducked away, past the stalls lining two sides of the street. What's wrong with that man? she wondered. As she hurried away, she smelled kusaya, small mackerel that were fermented and dried. It was the most disgusting food Aki could think of, reminding her of the odor of decaying garbage or the soiled socks of beggars. Usually, she held her breath as she walked by the stall, but she'd forgotten to avoid inhaling due to the shock of that awful fellow lunging at her.

Yuk, kusaya! Aki thought, running off.

The whole way home, she found it hard to shake off the feeling of revulsion. Only when Aki was back in her yard did the impression wear off.

Sticking her head into her hut, Aki found her mother at the kitchen stove.

"Welcome back, Aki," said Natsu, greeting her daughter. Leaning forward, Natsu was pouring a bucket of water into a large pot sitting over one of the circular openings above the fire box. The stove, built into the earthen floor, had a second opening at top, and another pot, this one covered with a lid, was sitting there with water waiting to boil.

As Aki lowered herself onto the bench outside the kitchen door, Natsu emerged and came to stand beside her daughter, asking, "How was your day?"

"Fine," Aki mumbled as she removed her sandals and slipped into her geta clogs.

The short reply seemed to satisfy Natsu. Humming a tune, Natsu began swaying back and forth. She stopped abruptly, remembering to ask, "Did you deliver the letters to Sister Bunkai?"

"I did," Aki answered before observing, "You're in a good mood, mom."

Smiling, Natsu lowered herself onto the bench next to her daughter and inquired, "And you saw Granny Mari?"

"Uh, huh."

"What did she have to say?"

"Well, she can't stop talking about the Gion Festival."

"Oh, right! She's a real fan."

"She's so excited," Aki agreed. Then she asked, "Which float will be at front on opening day, mom?"

"The Halberd float."

"Oh," Aki nodded.

Rising up from the bench, Natsu added, "Remember, Aki, we're taking baths before dinner."

"Right." Aki stood and grabbed her basket. "I'll be back in a bit."

Aki left to gather kindling for morning deliveries. She returned a half hour later and, grabbing a ball of twine, she wrapped three bundles of firewood. When she was finished with her chores, Aki stepped into the kitchen to help her mother carry two pots of heated water to a large wooden tub on a platform near their hut.

Natsu had already poured six large buckets of hot water into the nearly full tub. She pointed to a short wooden stool and told her daughter, "You go first, Aki."

Happy to comply, Aki removed her clothes and lowered herself onto the stool, where she picked up a pouch filled with rice bran and, using water from the tub, scrubbed her body clean. Meanwhile, Natsu poured one last bucket of hot water into the tub. Once she had rinsed off, Aki rose up from the stool and stepped gingerly into the hot water for a soak.

Peering down through the clear water, Aki examined her own naked body. Ripples in the water distorted her shape. The effect was fascinating. Aki smiled, but as her eyes came to focus on her chest, her expression changed.

Aki stared at the long crimson birthmark with a sigh. It never goes away, she thought. She remembered her mother saying that the mark didn't mean anything, and she shouldn't worry about it. But Aki couldn't ignore the fact that the mark was shaped like the written character for death, and it frightened those who saw it. Once, years earlier, she had been playing with other children in the village when her tunic had flown open at the front. Several mothers nearby had gasped and pulled their sons and daughters away. One had cried out, "That's the mark of death!" It seemed to Aki that those villagers had steered clear of her since then.

Maybe they're right, Aki said to herself, looking down at the birthmark. Mom's father and mother died a few days after I was born. And dad died when I was an infant. Maybe I'm the cause of all that bad luck.

For some reason, Aki now recalled the toothless fellow who had approached her outside the Yamabana Market. He had ogled her and called her sexy. What an awful guy, Aki thought, shaking her head. But I bet he would've run away screaming if he'd seen my birthmark!

Should I tell my mom about him? Aki wondered. No, I'm not going to, she decided. She'll just say I should ignore men like that.

"Here's your towel," said Natsu, approaching and handing her daughter a large rectangular sheet of loosely woven cotton.

After Aki had dried off and had slipped on her robe, she began running her fingers through the tangles in her wet hair. When a gentle breeze arose, she felt goosebumps prickling her skin. After a long, muggy day, it was a wonderful sensation.

"HERE AS ORDERED, SIR," ANNOUNCED A YOUNG RECRUIT before bowing deeply toward Ishida Kurōbei, the outlaw rōnin.

"Hm!" Kurōbei acknowledged, standing erect with his feet spread at the center of the barn, now a training facility for rōnin.

The recruit backed up several steps. He was still bent forward, holding his back flat with his torso parallel to the ground. When he straightened, he turned and took his place next to seven other recruits a short distance away. They waited at one shadowy side of the barn for Kurōbei to address them. The only sound was the buzzing of insects outside in the tall grass.

From the opposite side of the barn, three men now emerged, one wearing garments dyed rich maroon, another in chestnut brown and the third in pale indigo. The three marched forward and stood behind Kurōbei, facing the line of recruits. Responsible for instructing the recruits, they served as Kurōbei's trainers.

At last, Kurōbei began to speak, his voice sharp and imperious. "Less than a week from now, residents of Kyoto will launch their Gion Festival celebrations. Most of you recruits are new to Kyoto, so let me explain. What you will witness is Kyoto residents praying for a year free from pestilence. They will plead with the Ox-headed heavenly king for divine protection."

Kurōbei stopped abruptly. Then, placing his fists on his hips, he declared, "But the Heavenly king might not intercede on their behalf. He is angry! No, he is furious!"

Everything stopped, as if time stood still. Even the insects outside in the blinding sunlight ceased their humming. After a long pause, Kurōbei started up again.

"The Heavenly king must be placated. If he refuses to grant the people's entreaties, disaster will strike. Disease will spread, and many will die." Kurōbei turned and addressed the three sword instructors, looking for confirmation. "Is that not so, gentlemen?"

The instructors responded emphatically. "Yes, sir!"

Kurōbei turned back and went on, his voice rising. "What can we do to placate the Heavenly king? How do we avoid plague and illness?"

None of the men answered, each waiting for Kurōbei to answer his own questions.

"This is how—by attacking the source of the god's anger."

"Yes, sir," the instructors agreed, joined by the recruits.

Kurōbei continued. "We will demonstrate to the Heavenly king that we accept his terms for protection. We must call upon the shōgun to step aside. The Tokugawa brat must forfeit his claim to rulership of the realm."

"Yes," the instructors and recruits repeated, each stomping a foot in agreement.

Kurōbei gave a firm nod and continued. "The brat shōgun is a false ruler. We have no choice but to reject him."

"Reject him!" the men called out.

Even louder now, Kurōbei proclaimed, "We must venerate the emperor, not the shōgun. That's how it was in the ancient past, when our people lived together in harmony, free from disease and disorder."

"Yes!" the men called out as one.

As Kurōbei scanned the men's faces, moving from one to the next, each confirmed his agreement, declaring, "Yes, sir."

"The Heavenly king will not listen to the people's pleas unless *we* intercede," proclaimed Kurōbei. "It is up to us to strike down the ungodly shōgun. When the emperor is able to rule the realm once again, the Heavenly king will be placated. Only then can this truly be called the land of the gods."

"Yes!" the men clamored even more demonstrably.

Kurōbei paused, raising one arm to silence the men. Then he swiftly slashed the side of his hand diagonally through the air as he shouted, "The moment to strike is now. Do you agree?"

The men's voices rose up resoundingly. "Yes!"

Now Kurōbei changed his tone. He became calmer and his words more calculated. "I have devised a plan of action for the closing ceremony of the Gion Festival. We must send the Heavenly king a signal while he resides temporarily amongst us. Before he returns to the quiet of Gion Shrine, he must hear us."

The men nodded, waiting to hear more.

"I call on each of you to join me. Will you do your part to ensure the protection of the people of Kyoto? Will you pledge to unite with me in seizing this moment?"

All ten of the men called out their support. They were unanimous.

"We will usher in a glorious new age! The Heavenly king will protect us," Kurōbei stated confidently. Then he launched into a description of his plan, a public condemnation of the young Tokugawa shōgun and Elders on the Edo Central Council. It would be carried out in less than two weeks.

"Once I sell the rest of these greens, I'm leaving," announced Mari. She pointed a boney finger at a leafy mound. It was nearly the only fresh produce left on her counter at the Yamabana Market.

"You're going somewhere?" asked Aki, who had completed her deliveries and had come to the market to pick up provisions for Enshōji.

"Can you guess where, Little Aki?"

"Home?"

"No, you simpleton." Mari clicked her tongue. "I'm going to watch them set up Shinto floats for the festival."

"They're building the Gion floats already?"

Nodding and wiping her hands on her apron, Mari replied, "I'm sure they've started. I go watch every year. Have you ever seen it, Little Aki?"

"No." Aki shook her head.

"That's a shame. Zannen." As Mari grimaced, a network of wrinkles formed across her face. "Say, Miss Aki, you want to go with me?"

"I can't. I'm expected at the convent."

"Oh, of course. That reminds me, I've got their provisions packed and ready to go." Mari ducked down, reached under her counter and pulled out a bundle wrapped in a square of fabric. She pushed it across the counter, looking directly at Aki. "How about the parade of floats? Has your mother ever taken you to see that?"

"No. We're always too busy, but we went to see the opening procession once, when I was really young. I don't remember much except all the people and the noise."

"He, he!" cackled Mari. "So much commotion!"

"I remember those floats with the large dolls, though," Aki remarked. "Especially the floats with a doll placed in a pine tree on top of the roof—"

Mari interrupted excitedly. "Or bamboo!"

"Huh?"

"Some dolls are placed on a freshly-cut stalk of bamboo."

Mari's interest had been piqued, and she asked, "Do you remember the Mountain-grotto float, Little Aki? It's my favorite."

"No. Which god is it dedicated to?"

"Can't you guess, silly? Ha!" Mari responded loudly with a guffaw.

"Um—" Aki hesitated, feeling awkward. "No, I can't."

"Ha! It's dedicated to the god of the grotto, of course. He's enshrined inside the mound on that float. And the sun goddess and her brother are there, too."

"When the Mountain-grotto float approaches, the crowd roars. The gang of pullers drag it down the street with all their might. Those sure are some strong and handsome young men! No wonder the crowd cheers them on."

"Granny Mari, you know a lot about the Gion Festival," marveled Aki. "How about the parade of sacred palanquins. Have you ever seen that?"

Mari answered dismissively with a wave of her hand. "No. That starts late. Too late for me. I've got to get my beauty rest!"

"Uh, huh!" Aki was about to laugh but then thought better of it, seeing Mari's perfectly serious expression. "Is it true the carriers chant and sing to entertain the gods hidden inside the sacred palanquins?"

"Yes, it is. And the bells and rattles attached to each palanquin ring as the carriers rock it back and forth." Mari waved her hands back and forth. All that lively sound inspires the gods to help the townspeople. Well, that's what people say, anyway. And I believe them. But I got to tell you, Miss Aki—" Mari stopped and looked around. Then winking, she added in a whisper, "I think it's the men in their little tunics that inspire the gods. He! He!"

"Granny Mari!" Aki exclaimed, feeling uncomfortable. "Don't you think they wear those little tunics because it's hot parading through the streets? They're out for a long time, and they're carrying a heavy load."

"You're so serious, Little Aki—" Mari held off, seeing a young housewife approach.

The woman stopped at Mari's stall, commenting, "Those greens look fresh."

"They are!" Mari answered. "You can take them all. I'll give you a discount."

"Well—" the housewife hesitated.

"Oh! Come on. Just take them all. Feed them to your dog if you must."

"I don't have a dog," the woman mumbled.

Seeing Mari start to scoop up the spinach and turnip greens, Aki took the bundle of provision in her arms and said, "I better be going."

"Bye now," answered Mari.

Aki stepped away, saying, "Enjoy the floats, granny."

"I will!"

"How were your deliveries yesterday?" Bunkai asked, setting down her writing brush.

"Good," replied Aki, who had just entered the Ryokuin'an study. After greeting her teacher and taking her seat, Aki noticed a poem scroll had been laid out for her to copy.

"Aki, did you stop at each of the spots we discussed?" Bunkai asked.

"Yes, Sister Bunkai. I dropped off a bundle of kindling with a secret letter at the Nagataniden, the Shōgōin and the Jissōin. But I didn't find letters to bring back from any of those places."

"That's alright. On some days, it'll be like that. Tomorrow morning, I'll give you letters for the Ichijō, Nijō and Hachijō residences. Understood?"

"Yes, Sister Bunkai. But—"

"But what, Aki?"

"Can't the convent manservant deliver the secret letters?"

"No. We once had him deliver letters for us, but not any longer. Prince Toshitada and the Manshuin abbot agree with me that the manservant would be recognized and that you're the best choice for the job now, Aki."

"Oh! I'm happy to carry the letters, Sister Bunkai. I just thought you wanted me to do something risky."

"It *is* risky. Abunai desu yo!" Bunkai warned. "Rogues make their living by preying on innocent women in town. I greatly regret putting you in harm's way."

"But my mother taught me how to be careful when I started delivering firewood years ago."

"And now you have special letters to protect. They put you in even greater danger, Aki."

"Really? What's in the letters?" Aki said, knowing immediately she shouldn't have asked.

Frowning, Bunkai shook her head. "I don't know, Aki. I should warn you not to try opening one of the letters. You'd have to break the seal, and the damage would be obvious."

"I wouldn't do that, Sister Bunkai. And I'll be careful. I promise."

"Good. Now, how about starting your lesson, Aki?"

Aki nodded and turned her attention to her work. She prepared ink, took a sheet of paper, smoothed it out on her desktop and picked up a writing brush. For the remainder of the morning, she remained quiet wondering what was written in the letters she carried. Aki couldn't help but be curious. What kind of secrets do those aristocrats and clerics have anyway? she wondered.

When the time came for communal prayers at the convent, the two women finished their work and began cleaning up their desks. As they stood to leave, Bunkai inquired, "What's your plan for the afternoon, Aki?"

Following her teacher through the doorway and onto the front veranda of the Ryokuin'an, Aki answered, "I think

I'll take a walk south and visit the temple of Jishōji. I've never seen the Silver Pavilion there."

"Ah! Good idea. With the crush of the Gion Festival, it's probably best to avoid the downtown streets," remarked Bunkai, as she led the way down the steps to the convent courtyard. Then she stopped, saying, "You know, the Silver Pavilion isn't actually covered with silver. A shōgun built it as a worship hall for his retirement villa. They say he meant to add thin sheets of silver to the exterior, but he changed his mind."

Her interest aroused, Aki bowed and thanked her teacher before saying goodbye and heading off. As she walked downhill toward town, she recalled her teacher's warning. She shook her head, thinking, I'm not worried. I can watch out for thieves. It's simple enough.

Along the way, the fields gave way to houses with side yards and then to townhouses with gardens in the rear. The streets grew warmer and, by the time Aki reached Jishōji, she was sweating. She stopped in a shady spot outside the temple entrance to read a placard explaining the temple's past. Then she entered the grounds and toured the landscaped gardens. Avoiding the glare off the pond, she turned back time and again to view the two-story pavilion. Each time she stopped to look, the scene appeared differently.

After a long stretch, she followed the path to the gate and left the temple precinct. Once outside, Aki headed straight toward a row of shops she had spotted earlier. She ducked into the dark interior of a small souvenir concession crammed with items for sale, everything from rice crackers to teapots. Standing near the entrance, she picked up a familiar toy, a hand game with a cup and a ball. She tried it out, scooping the ball into the cup. Then she moved on to examine spinning tops and wooden dolls. Soon, she was stepping farther into the shop to browse a row of wind chimes.

The chimes were for hanging outdoors under the eaves. Many were colorful and shiny. A few, sitting at the far end of the row, were more subdued. One caught her eye. The exterior surface resembled the hull of a roasted chestnut. Suspended from its clapper was a slip of tinted paper with a frolicking rabbit dashed off in ink.

Sister Bunkai would love this! Aki decided. Aki picked up the chime and presented it to the proprietress, standing nearby.

"I'll take this. Would you put it in a sheet of that paper?" Aki pointed to a stack of saffron-colored wrapping paper behind the counter.

"Certainly, young lady," the shopkeeper replied. "Is this a gift for someone special?"

"Yes. It's for my teacher. I take lessons at the convent of Enshōji." Aki stopped. She hoped the shopkeeper hadn't detected a note of pride in her voice.

"Is that so? Is the convent near here?" asked the shopkeeper as she nestled the chime in a mound of paper.

"Umm—no. Enshōji is up north." Aki dropped her head and removed two coins from her purse, placing them on the counter.

Seems the shopkeeper hasn't even heard of Enshōji, Aki said to herself. I guess people in town aren't familiar with the convent. It's too remote.

Just as Aki was reaching out to take the package from the shopkeeper, something brushed her elbow, and she realized that someone had approached her from behind. With a quick glance over her shoulder, she saw it was a man, a burly fellow with a scarf wrapped around his head. He peeked over Aki's shoulder at the package in her hands and walked away.

After thanking the shopkeeper, Aki moved toward the doorway. Suddenly, the burly fellow appeared in front of her. She noticed now that the hair at the nape of the man's neck was flecked with grey and that he was holding a cane. Stepping over the threshold before her, the man lost his footing. His cane went flying, and he tumbled into the roadway. Several people outside witnessed the fall, but no one stopped.

"Can I help you, sir?" Aki offered, bending down and reaching out her hand to assist the man.

"Ah! You're very kind, young lady." The man took her hand and stood up awkwardly, brushing the dust from his leggings. "My legs are unsteady these days. Mind helping me a bit more?"

"Of course not," Aki answered.

"Could you take me to that bench—the one in the shade?"

"Oh! Sure," Aki responded, tucking the gift for Bunkai into her wide kimono sleeve and picking up the man's cane from the roadside. She grabbed the man's elbow, led him to the bench and waited as he took a seat at one end.

Casting a quick inquiring glance at the man, she said, "Can I be of any further assistance, sir?"

He rubbed the back of his neck and mumbled weakly, "If I sit here and rest a moment, I should be able to make it home on my own."

Aki sensed the fellow might be feebler than he looked. She wondered what to do.

"Young lady, I do believe I'll be fine with a little rest. But perhaps you'd be so kind as to stay with me for a few minutes just in case."

"Well—sure." Aki lowered herself onto the empty spot on the bench.

"Let me introduce myself. My name is Gohei. I've recently returned to Kyoto. I was away for a number of years. Unfortunately, my lower back and my legs cause me trouble."

"Ah!" Aki replied nervously, kicking the tip of her sandal against a cobblestone. "I mean, nice to meet you, Mister Gohei."

Gohei dipped his head with a smile, wrinkles forming around his eyes. He said, "Guess where I'm going."

Aki tilted her head and replied, "Downtown? Are you going to watch them set up the Gion floats?"

"No." Gohei shook his head. "I'm going to watch the new kabuki performance at Minamiza Theater. I already saw it once, but I've *got* to go again. Did anyone tell you about it?"

Aki shook her head, asking, "You like kabuki plays?"

"I sure do. I'm not such an old fart." Gohei made a silly face.

When Aki let out a laugh, the man smiled.

"Kabuki plays appeal to everyone, and Kyoto folk are inspired. That's what I say. No one can stop their creativity.

Like seeds planted in wet spring soil that give rise to summer flowers."

Aki nodded, feeling a bit uncertain. She'd never heard that phrase before.

"The new play is set at an Inari shrine. Young miss, did you know—the Inari deity protects warriors, including rōnin?"

Aki shook her head.

Gohei started up again. "I'm sorry—I'm going on and on without asking about you. Why not tell me about yourself? Judging from your clothing, I'd say you live in the foothills. Delivery woman, are you? You carry flowers into town every morning?"

Aki shook her head. "My mother delivers flowers. I deliver kindling. Today is my day off."

"Good for you! Everyone deserves a day off now and then. Ha, ha!"

Aki looked off down the roadway, feeling uncertain. It's strange sitting so close to a total stranger, she thought. Mister Gohei seems stronger, now. He's even laughing. Can I leave now? she wondered.

Without another word, Aki jumped up, saying, "Excuse me, sir, but I'm afraid I need to go." With that, she dashed off.

Upon reaching the end of the temple lane, Aki headed northward. After several minutes, she slowed, remembering Bunkai's gift. Checking inside her sleeve, she found it there, tucked away safely.

Taking her time, Aki walked up Shirakawa Avenue and, after crossing the Otowa River, she followed the Shugakuin road to the mountain path and then into the forested slopes, thankful for a cool afternoon breeze. When she saw ahead of her a favorite landmark on the mountainside—a majestic cedar tree—she slowed. Attached to the trunk were long strips of bark in rusty red and burnt umber. The strips of bark reached down to a lush carpet of emerald green moss that enveloped the cedar's knobby roots. Aki brought her hands together and bowed her head. Around the tree's thick trunk, someone had wrapped a wide straw rope with folded strips of paper attached, indicating that others also worshipped the tree.

Aki started up again and, before long, she caught sight of the last bend in the trail. Just beyond, she spied a thin, white ribbon rising above the tree line and twisting into the sky. She sighed, knowing that it came from the smoke hole in the roof of her hut and indicated her mother had returned and had started a fire in their kitchen stove. Soon, Aki was home again, too.

"STAY CLOSE," BARKED KURŌBEI. HE WAS WEARING HIS BLACK lacquered hat and had a pair of swords tucked into the sash around his hips. Moving with youthful vigor, the rōnin led five of his recruits through the dense throng in downtown Kyoto.

The recruits followed Kurōbei as the crowd, which had gathered at the intersection of Fourth Street and Karasuma Avenue, swarmed around them. The crowd was waiting with mounting excitement for the Gion floats to start moving.

After delivering a sharp kick to a spectator's shin, Kurōbei stepped forward. Turning back to the recruits, he ordered, "Push your way to the front."

"Yes, sir," the five recruits called out, advancing in Kurōbei's wake.

Now the rōnin outlaw stopped. To his right, a man lifted onto his shoulders a young boy, who was fingering a shrine amulet made from woven blades of bamboo grass.

"What's that, papa?" The boy pointed a pudgy finger toward a leafy sprig atop the peaked roof of a nearby float.

"It's a sacred tree," the father replied.

"A tree?" the boy asked.

"Uh, huh. The gods come down from the heavens to sit in the tree and protect us from the evil spirits that cause sickness—" The father stopped abruptly and winced as he felt someone stepping on one of his big toes. Pulling his foot back, the father lost his place at the front of the crowd, while Kurōbei pushed ahead, replacing him.

Kurōbei kept moving, snaking around in the crowd with his five recruits struggling to keep up. Another ten steps, and Kurōbei gestured with his chin to something down the street, saying, "There it is—the Halberd float. It's got a tall lance on top. See it?"

"Yes, sir," answered the recruits, squinting at the float with a large-scale replica of a pole weapon projecting upward from its central mast.

Kurōbei advanced toward the Halberd float and, coming to a halt close to it, he extended his elbows out to avoid being jostled by the crowd. Stopping behind him, the recruits assumed identical stances.

"Take a good look at the float's design," commanded Kurōbei. "The Halberd float leads the procession today. A week from now, it'll be at the back."

"Yes, sir," responded the recruits as they examined the Halberd float.

Kurōbei proceeded to explain, "Each wheeled float has two leaders who'll hang onto ropes at the front as the float moves forward."

The recruits nodded.

"When necessary, they use wedges to stop the float."

The recruits nodded again.

"Notice the boys sitting under the roof on the second level. The one in the middle is the sacred child." Kurōbei pointed at three figures atop the float, boys with fine robes and white powdered faces. The middle boy wore a golden mantle and a phoenix crown.

Kurōbei continued, saying, "Any minute now, that sacred child will cut the straw rope to start the event. Then he'll dance as he beats a drum, keeping time for the musicians behind him."

The recruits gave another nod.

"Once the sacred child cuts the rope, the floats will start moving and the crowd will surge forward with the floats."

The recruits nodded yet again.

"The procession heads east from here and turns right at Teramachi to head south. At Matsubara, it'll turn right again and continue on westward. The whole route takes three hours to complete. Understood?"

"Understood, sir."

Glaring, Kurōbei added, "Keep track of where you are. If we get separated, meet me back at the barn by noon."

"Yes, sir."

A murmur arose from the crowd, and the group of rōnin lifted their gaze.

The sacred boy on the Halberd float had wrapped his hands around the hilt of his sword and now lifted the blade overhead, pointing it at a straw rope hanging across the street directly in front of him. When the boy swung the sword, the rope fell away toward the two sides of the street. At that moment, a cacophony erupted. Flutes, gongs, cymbals and drums joined together with revelers' voices raised in song and laughter. Gion festival music proclaimed the start of the parade, which now swept everyone up in an eastward surge.

Kurōbei watched as the leaders on the Halberd float yelled out to the gang of men pulling the float forward in the street. Each of the leaders used a fan to signal and direct the pullers.

After several minutes of bumping and shoving, Kurōbei looked over his shoulder to see a throng of animated figures. His recruits were not among them, though. He shrugged and continued on with the crowd.

A KITCHEN MAID

At last! Aki said to herself.

Spotting the plastered wall at the south side of the Konoe estate, Aki turned, leaving the main road and entering the alleyway that separated two aristocratic residences. Aki headed down the narrow path toward the Konoe kitchen, preparing to make her final kindling delivery of the morning. Ahead, she saw a thin, young woman in a wrinkled shift and a maid's apron.

Aki stopped to watch the young maid creep along, hugging the Konoe wall. Suddenly, the maid darted across the alley, pulled something from her sleeve and tossed it into the bushes.

Hearing a munching sound, Aki noticed movement in the bushes and a black nose emerging from the leafy branches. That maid's feeding a dog, Aki realized. Advancing toward the young woman, Aki called out, "Hello!"

The maid jumped up and spun around. Then, dropping her head, she mumbled, "I'm sorry."

"Don't worry," Aki remarked, seeing the maid's miserable expression.

"I didn't mean to cause a problem," the maid went on, now with a pout on her pock-marked face. "No one's fed the dogs in days. They're just so hungry. Peko, peko!"

Realizing that the maid must be disobeying someone's orders, Aki repeated, "Don't worry."

"If I'm found out, I'll be dismissed," the maid whimpered. "Please don't tell anyone. I'll give you something from the kitchen if you promise to keep it to yourself."

"I'll stay quiet," Aki replied. "But to be honest, I don't want anything from your kitchen. Thanks anyway. Did someone tell you not to feed the dogs?"

The maid grimaced and explained, "The head cook ordered me not to when he listed all the rules here. I started working in the kitchen not too long ago."

"I won't say anything," Aki promised.

The maid broke into a sudden smile. "Oh good! As thanks, I'll tell you a secret."

"I always like a secret," Aki replied, intending her comment to be funny.

Taking her seriously, the maid stepped closer and said under her breath, "Alright. I've got all kinds of secrets."

Aki remained silent, taken aback by the young woman's abrupt transformation from a cringing maid into a keen gossip.

The maid gestured for Aki to follow her up the alley. Halting, she turned back to face Aki, asking, "What do you want to know?"

Aki removed the kindling from her head, straightened her garments, thought for a moment and replied, "Well, can you tell me anything about the thief called Shining Blade?"

"Sure. He's been spotted near Yamabana Market."

"No! Where did you hear that?"

"I hear all kinds of things in the Konoe mansion," the maid answered, no longer whispering. "I catch lots of secrets when I'm cleaning with the other servants or when I'm delivering trays to the dining room."

Looking at the maid sideways, Aki replied, "Really?"

"Uh, huh. Say, I'm Sumi. What's your name?"

"I'm Aki."

"So, Sister Aki, like I was about to say—Shining Blade's been showing his face around town. A few weeks ago, he killed the gate attendant at the Nijō residence. That's just a few blocks from here. And it's only a short distance from the emperor's palace. Shining Blade is so daring."

"Daring?" Aki responded, observing Sumi cautiously.

"They say he's sly," Sumi continued. "He's a true master with the sword. He's nineteen, like me, but he already has wounds from his swordfights."

"Hmm," Aki murmured. "You're nineteen?"

"Well, more like seventeen. But I'm mature for my age."

"Really!"

"I bet Shining Blade is handsome," Sumi exclaimed. "Maybe as handsome as those men pulling the Halberd Float. Did you get a look at them!"

"I saw the floats—" Aki stopped, interrupted by Sumi.

"No, not the floats, silly! The men. They're really something! They're hunkier than warriors."

"Warriors?" Aki shot Sumi another sideways glance.

"Uh, huh! What? I suppose you prefer gnarled-up monks and awful old priests!"

"Well—" Aki hesitated. "I think temples and shrines are nice. They're places where people can go to escape the violence of the world of warriors."

"You can't be serious, Sister Aki! I'd love to get mixed up in the world of warriors. Those men with swords—they're so strong." Sumi pulled on Aki's sleeve, adding, "And fascinating!"

"Fascinating? The world of warriors is frightening."

"No, really!" Sumi dropped her jaw and let her mouth hang open, as she raised a hand to each of her checks mockingly.

"Stop that!" Aki wasn't impressed.

"Well, at least the world of warriors isn't all drudgery like mine is. I'm wasting my life in a kitchen. Collecting slops and scrubbing pots—that's what I got to look forward to." Sumi twisted her mouth in frustration.

Beginning to sympathize with the young maid, Aki changed her tone. "I enjoy working at the stove. Don't you?"

"I don't get to cook," Sumi answered, sounding peeved. "I liked it better when I helped as a house maid. Now all I do is clean up and finish other stupid chores. I'm stuck working here—it's so boring."

"That sounds bad, Miss Sumi," Aki commiserated.

"Anyway, warriors are good looking! And so are rōnin—like that guy Shining Blade. I bet he's really handsome."

"Handsome? I heard he's got a big scar on his face," Aki retorted.

"Sounds interesting!"

Aki shrugged, deciding to move on. "So, I thought you were going to tell me some good secrets, Miss Sumi."

"Sure. Alright. What can I tell you?"

"How about this—do you know why the shōgun made the retired emperor marry his daughter?"

"What? Is that some kind of riddle? Like—There once was a shōgun. He made the emperor marry his daughter. Then what?"

"No! The second Tokugawa shōgun made the emperor marry his daughter—do you know anything about *that*?"

"How could I know anything about that?" Sumi snapped at Aki. "Stop asking stupid questions."

Aki clamped her mouth shut, afraid of uttering something she shouldn't.

Sumi quickly perked up, suggesting, "I can tell you about the festival floats. I learned all about them the last couple days."

"Really? Are the—"

Sumi interrupted yet again, unable to contain her sudden enthusiasm. "Did you know, Miss Aki, they don't use nails to build the floats, even the biggest ones? They use wooden pegs and straw ropes to build those big box-like structures."

"So, how do they build—" Aki stopped as Sumi jumped back in.

"First, the workers go to the storage barns down at Fourth and Karasuma. They drag the wooden poles and planks out and stack them into wagons. They pull the wagons to their spot in line and unload the float parts. It's unbelievable how quickly they can get a float together."

"Huh!"

"Some of the pieces are huge! The two-story floats with big wheels have a massive central pole. I bet it's as tall as Yasaka pagoda. Or—" Sumi hesitated and amended her statement. "Maybe it's not quite that tall."

Aki nodded, hoping to hear more.

"And did you know it takes thirty or forty men to pull just one of those two-story floats?"

"Well—" Aki stopped and, realizing Sumi might actually allow her to finish a sentence, she remarked, "I heard how they turn the wheeled floats at intersections. It's really strange."

"Oh! Those wheeled floats can only go straight! When they need to turn a corner, everyone comes to a halt, and they put bamboo poles down flat on the ground. They pour water on the poles and slowly turn the float. You've seen it, right?"

Before Aki could respond, a man with a shiny head emerged from the Konoe side gate. Then he ducked back into the compound.

"Uh, oh!" Sumi mumbled, having seen the man. "I should be going before that cross-eyed monster comes to get me."

"Alright," Aki replied, bending forward to pick up her bundle of firewood. By the time she had returned upright, Sumi was gone.

When a minute had passed, Aki followed. She entered the empty Konoe kitchen courtyard, where she placed the firewood on the ground near the doorway. Then she approached a blue-lidded ceramic pot sitting on a stoop. She bent down to check inside for letters. Seeing none, she replaced the lid.

Now hearing a creak, Aki looked up to see a completely bald man standing in the kitchen doorway. When he turned to stare in her direction, Aki noticed his eyes seemed to focus on something at the tip of his nose. Hurrying off through the gate and down the alleyway, she heard a man's sharp voice behind her. Aki turned, but no one was there. She guessed it had been the man she'd just encountered, although she was too far away to make out what he'd said.

Was he talking to me? Aki wondered, leaving the alley and entering the main roadway. Rejoining the pedestrian traffic heading eastward, Aki began considering Sumi, the chatty maid. Sumi sure knows a lot, Aki thought. She's a pot of gold.

KURŌBEI STRIKES

"Here comes another float!" announced the party host, one of Kyoto's many prosperous merchants. The host was busy entertaining seven guests in the second-story viewing gallery of his townhouse at the heart of Kyoto. He mingled casually with the row of seated men who were observing the procession of floats in the street below.

"Ah, yes," responded a pair of young courtiers. They had joined other prestigious invitees at the host's home, a townhouse located on Teramachi Avenue just south of Fourth Street. The guests had gathered to view the closing procession of floats celebrating the finale of the Gion Festival, a grand spectacle.

Earlier that morning, the homeowner had ordered servants to open sliding doors in his second-story rooms that faced the street. Then he had overseen servants hanging curtains below the eaves and pulling them partially aside. Once that was done, he had watched as servants laid out cushions inside the railing. Several hours later, the host had greeted his guests, including several senior representatives of the Edo government.

One of the guests was the Kyoto governor, Itakura Shigemune, who wore garments of lustrous, dark blue silk with a lozenge pattern. The governor had been ushered to the prime viewing spot at the center of the viewing gallery. In his late sixties, Itakura had thinning hair and worry lines running across his forehead. His bad back caused him to pitch forward slightly. Sitting beside the governor was another senior official, the Second Street magistrate, Gomi Toyonao. Older and taller than Itakura, Gomi was thin with a thick, gray mustache, and he wore a robe of fine brown cotton.

Now, as a towering float came into view, a chorus of "Ahs!" rose up from the crowded street below.

The host identified the approaching vehicle, announcing for all to hear, "The Renunciate's float!"

"It's taller than I remember," remarked one of the gentlemen in the gallery.

Another, the youngest man in the party, queried, "Where's the figure of the renunciate monk?"

"He's there, a bit to the left," the host answered, standing at the rear and leaning forward as he pointed out the monastic figure on the float. Turning to the gentleman, who was enjoying his first chance to see the parade from on high, the host added, "And see the ornament at the top representing the sun, the moon and the stars, your excellency?"

"Ah, yes! I see it. Just as they say, it's got three joined disks."

"Indeed," the host remarked. "Light from those celestial bodies shines down on all of us. And the soaring pole at the center of the float points to the heavens."

"That's wonderful!" the young courtier responded, before a wall of sound drowned him out. With musical instruments blaring, the men directing the float shouted to the pullers dragging the massive structure forward.

After the float had passed directly in front of the viewing gallery, the host stood and left his guests. He reappeared a minute later holding a gourd in one hand and a spouted ceramic vessel in the other. He approached his guests from behind, offering drinks. "More saké, gentlemen? Or some strong tea to accompany your rice cakes?"

"You are a most generous host," one of the courtiers remarked, lifting his saké cup for a refill.

The host poured rice wine from the gourd, telling the courtiers, "There's more to come at lunchtime, gentlemen. We've got cold noodles and chimaki." After that, the homeowner turned to another guest, suggesting a refill.

"Yes, certainly," the man replied, also raising his cup.

The homeowner poured the man his saké before dispensing some for himself. Lifting his cup, he toasted the guests with a "Kanpai." The guests saluted him in return and quickly downed their drinks. Then the host moved toward the governor, who was peering into the street below. The governor accepted a cup of tea, as did the magistrate beside him.

Once the homeowner had poured drinks for all of his guests, he set down his saké gourd and teapot and began singing a lively tune. Several guests joined in. In their revelry, no one seemed to notice a newcomer enter the viewing gallery. He was a well-groomed man in uniform—Deputy Inspector Tanaka.

Tanaka advanced toward the two high Edo officials to inform them of his arrival. Bowing deeply, he greeted Governor Itakura first.

The governor glanced over his shoulder and, seeing Tanaka, he dipped his head slightly. Then he turned to Magistrate Gomi and inquired tersely, "Where is Wada?"

"Commissioner Wada is out of town, your excellency," answered Gomi, his voice raspy. "I ordered Deputy Inspector Tanaka to report in his place."

"I see." Itakura gave another quick nod.

Next Tanaka moved a step to the right behind Magistrate Gomi and bowed again. He leaned toward the magistrate, cupped his hand around his mouth and whispered, "Excuse me, sir."

Meanwhile a troop of dancers had marched forward in the street below, stopping directly in front of the governor. They had bowed toward the gallery and had taken their positions to perform. Gomi gestured for Tanaka to hold off. The dancers started singing boisterously to percussion accompaniment, making it impossible for Tanaka to hear anything more the magistrate might say.

Tanaka stood erect, planted his feet and waited. A few minutes later, when the raucous troop had finished their performance and had moved on, Tanaka took advantage of the receding noise. He leaned toward Gomi again and asked, "Sir, your orders?"

Without taking his eyes from the crowd below him, the magistrate issued instructions. "Take two of your men and join the soldiers stationed below. Stand watch over the officials sitting opposite us at street level. Keep your eyes on the governor up in this gallery, as well. Stop anyone attempting to force their way in."

"Yes, sir."

Tanaka left, finding his way down the stairs and into the congested street, where he located two of his agents, The Wolf and The Crab. After ordering The Crab to stand with the soldier who guarded the townhouse entrance, he signaled The Wolf to follow him. Crossing the street, he took up a position between two rows of tatami mats. The mats had been pulled out from indoors, placed at the sides of Teramachi Street and covered with red felt. Officials working for the magistrate had claimed spots on the mats and chatted with their neighbors. Some sat cross-legged, and others squatted with one knee up. A serving boy was offering the men pieces of roasted squash on a plate.

Tanaka turned to The Wolf with directions. "You take up a position here. I'll go down the street a ways. Keep your eyes on the governor."

The Wolf nodded, going to stand behind the officials.

The deputy inspector walked several doors down and, stepping into a shadowy corner, checked to ensure his view. From this vantage point, he could see the governor and the commissioner in the gallery above, as well as the officials sitting at street level. He could also see The Wolf to his far left and The Crab at the entrance to the townhouse.

Tanaka settled back into his spot and scanned the crowd. Then he looked up into the second-story gallery. The homeowner had resumed serving saké and tea. It's going well, Tanaka decided. Everyone looks happy and relaxed. Turning his eyes back to the street, Tanaka examined the vendors moving up and down facing the revelers. One vendor called out, "Skewers of green pepper," while another intoned, "Fried balls of battered octopus."

Now a group of five musicians carrying hand drums arrived on foot and stopped in front of the viewing gallery. Accompanying them was a pair of male performers, who each wore a tall headdress shaped like the head of a long-necked bird. Specializing in the dance of the hernshaws, they wore white garments with a strand with long silk feathers wrapped around their necks and tied loosely under their chins.

"We're here to beseech the gods to protect us from harm," announced one of the dancers as he and his companion began to move to the accompaniment of the drummers. Reaching their arms to the side, the dancers' feathers extended outward like the wings of a white heron. Gasps of "Oh!" and "Ah!" rose up from the crowd.

Once the hernshaw dancers had moved on, the vendors and the revelers began thinning out, signaling a lull in the procession. Tanaka stayed where he was, examining the members of the magistrate's office sitting streetside, some eating and drinking, others playing go and other board games. Tanaka glanced back up into the gallery, observing the governor and the magistrate in conversation. As the host arrived with bowls of cold noodles, they held off and accepted a bowl each.

Tanaka lowered his eyes once more to the street where people milled around, waiting for the arrival of the Halberd float, the last spectacle of the procession. When Tanaka shot The Wolf a questioning glance, The Wolf responded by signaling an all's well.

Tanaka moved closer to The Wolf to listen in on two officials seated nearby. One was a man of ample proportions, and the other was a young visitor from Edo. The visitor commented, "I heard the Halberd float goes way back to a time when the emperor called on men to march from Gion Shrine to the imperial gardens. But I suppose there's more to the story."

"Most definitely. You're not from here, so let me explain," answered the heavyset man, speaking in a high-pitched, officious manner. "Sixty-six men marched to the gardens. Each carried a halberd representing one of the sixty-six provinces of the realm. While the people sang and danced, the plague spirits came and congregated on the halberds. The evil spirits were then carried away from town, after which the halberds were destroyed."

The Edo visitor nodded with a sigh and an expression of flagging interest.

The man declared, "To this very day, people make the pilgrimage to Gion Shrine to pray to the Ox-headed heavenly king, beseeching him to vanquish the plague spirits."

Still nodding, the visitor stifled a yawn.

"Oh! Wait!" exclaimed the corpulent man. "Here comes another of the wheeled floats."

The two officials turned their attention to a mast in the distance, soaring over the mob of pullers and musicians marching toward them. The mast was a gigantic replica of a pole weapon surmounting the Halberd float. A loud cheer rose up from the crowd, enthralled by the height of the

Halberd float and the brilliantly colored embellishments on its sides. Then lively music erupted and swept down the street.

Those lingering in the middle of Teramachi Avenue scurried away, allowing the troop accompanying the Halberd float to move forward. Leaders shouted out, hanging onto ropes while waving their fans and directing the pullers. The muscles of the pullers bulged as they strained to drag the weighty float forward.

Although he had seen the parade every year since being hired by the Office of the Kyoto Governor, Tanaka was stirred yet again by the enormity of the Halberd float. Staring at its approach, Tanaka realized that his view of Governor Itakura and Magistrate Gomi would be blocked when the float came within an arm's reach of him. Tanaka prepared to step to the side, but just then he noticed something odd. The curtains covering the float's lower level were parting very slightly, and something was emerging.

Is that someone's hand? Tanaka asked himself. Yes, it *is*, he realized. What's it holding? Maybe a rolled-up scroll. Wait! There's someone behind the curtain who just launched a scroll toward us.

Tanaka leaped into action. As the scroll went sailing through the air, the deputy inspector jumped past the two officials sitting closest to him. He was only a step away when the scroll hit the ground. Reaching it in mere seconds, Tanaka bent forward and picked it up. Then, as he began standing upright, Tanaka's eyes were drawn to the second story of the townhouse across from him. Something was happening in the viewing gallery. Three gentlemen were standing and gesticulating, while others looked on in surprise. The homeowner lifted an object overhead. It was a scroll, the same size as the one in Tanaka's hand.

Tanaka dashed across the street with The Wolf at his heels. The Crab joined them as they sprinted into the host's residence and up the stairs to the viewing gallery. The agents stopped at the top of the stairs to take in the scene. Tanaka tucked his scroll into the back of his sash and stepped forward. He watched Magistrate Gomi turn to Governor Itakura, asking, "Have you been harmed, sir?"

When the governor shook his head, Tanaka took a step back and addressed The Wolf and The Crab under his breath. "Chase after the Halberd float. Check whether anything is amiss. Examine the interior of that float, under the fabric curtains. Look for any sign of someone having infiltrated that area. Meet me back at the townhouse entrance when you have concluded your investigation."

"Yes, sir," replied the two agents, setting off straightaway.

Tanaka turned, hearing the homeowner behind him.

The homeowner declared, "Governor Itakura, your name is written here on the outside of the scroll. It seems to be a message addressed to you."

Gomi gestured for Tanaka to take the scroll from the homeowner. Tanaka did as he was ordered.

Leaning to the side, Gomi said something into the ear of the governor. Then standing, Gomi left his seat and whispered to the homeowner. Responding immediately, the homeowner stepped into the townhouse interior, leading the governor and Gomi into a private room. Tanaka followed. The other guests stayed behind, whispering amongst themselves.

"Your excellencies, please make yourselves comfortable here," the host said to Governor Itakura and Magistrate Gomi. Then he bowed and left the room, closing the door behind him.

Itakura lowered himself onto a cushion, squared his shoulders and turned to Gomi, saying, "Open the scroll and tell me what it says."

Gomi took a seat, unwound the silk cord wrapped around the scroll and rolled the scroll open. He started in, reading out loud, "The true followers of his majesty Emperor GoKōmyō call on Governor Itakura and all other Edo authorities to leave Kyoto immediately—"

"Leave Kyoto!" Itakura repeated in dismay.

"Yes, sir. There's more."

"Read it!" Itakura commanded with a scowl.

"Yes, sir." Gomi continued. "The young shōgun and the Edo Central Council are agents of disease and disorder. The Heavenly king will not protect the people if warrior usurpers dominate the ancient capital. The realm of the gods must be purified. The unholy influence of the Edo Elders and the false boy shōgun must end. Do not delay or we will attack."

The room became quiet as Gomi slowly rolled the scroll back up and wound the cord around to secure it.

The governor broke the silence, inquiring sharply, "Who's behind this?"

"Your excellency—" Gomi paused. "Ishida Kurōbei might be involved."

"That young rōnin criminal?" the governor demanded to know.

"Yes, sir," answered Gomi. "The one who calls himself Shining Blade. We've been pursuing him for over a month, sir."

"Any idea how he managed this stunt?"

Gomi turned to Tanaka, who was standing at the top of the stairs, and gestured for him to answer the governor's question.

Tanaka took a step forward, stating, "Governor Itakura, I believe Kurōbei and one or more of his rōnin followers used the Halberd float to hide in. They must have planned their action in order to throw the scroll into the viewing gallery. I have agents investigating the matter as we speak, sir."

Scowling, Itakura ordered, "Send me a report as soon as you learn anything."

"Yes, sir." Tanaka dipped his head.

Sitting up straight, the governor added, "That is all for now. The procession has concluded."

"Yes, sir," Gomi and Tanaka replied in unison.

Itakura turned to Gomi with an order. "Call for my palanquin. I will return to my office."

Gomi left the room and returned shortly with two guards to usher the governor down the stairs. Gomi and Tanaka remained behind, bent at the waist and bowing toward the retreating figures.

Once the governor had disappeared, the two men returned upright, and Tanaka interjected, "A question, if I may, Magistrate Gomi."

"What's that?" Gomi replied tersely.

"Sir, should I contact Commissioner Wada and request that he return?" inquired Tanaka.

"No. Wada will not be returning to Kyoto anytime soon. I will inform him of what happened here. Consider yourself fully vested with the authority to pursue and arrest Ishida Kurōbei."

"Yes, sir." Tanaka began lowering his head but quickly lifted it again. "Another thing, sir. There was a second scroll. It landed in the street below."

Tanaka reached back and under his sash to remove the second scroll, the one he had personally retrieved. He had meant to give it to the magistrate when he'd first returned to the viewing gallery, but in the confusion he'd lost track.

"Open it," Gomi ordered.

Tanaka dipped his head, opened the second scroll and quietly read what was written there. The contents were identical to those in the scroll thrown toward the governor. "It's the same, sir."

"Hmm," Gomi mumbled. Handing Tanaka the first scroll, which he was still holding, he said, "Take those back to your office and study them, deputy inspector. Write a report concerning what you observed here. I will contact you again soon."

"Yes, sir," Tanaka replied, as he slipped the scrolls up his sleeve.

"That is all for now, deputy inspector."

After bowing deeply, Tanaka turned, descended the stairs and left the townhouse. He waited in the street for his two agents to return. Looking around, he noticed that most of the activity in the street had died down.

Why two scrolls? Tanaka wondered. Was the second scroll a backup, in case the first scroll didn't reach the viewing gallery? If so, thought Tanaka, it was misfired and ended up in the street. Or perhaps the second scroll had intentionally been thrown into the street for the officials to find. Those officials would have read the contents and spread the word, making it impossible for the governor to cover up the incident. That must be it! Tanaka realized. The second scroll was meant to warn the gathered officials they are as vulnerable as the governor and the magistrate. The rōnin perpetrators meant to forewarn all the Edo officials.

"Another scorcher," declared Mari, the frizzy-haired stall keeper. She was standing behind her vegetable counter at the far side of the Yamabana Market.

"Sure is! Atsui," agreed Aki as she stopped to pull a handkerchief from under her sash and wipe the sweat from her forehead. She had spent the morning trudging down sweltering streets and dropping off firewood in steamy courtyards. She felt she would suffocate under all her delivery gear. Even though her jacket was light-weight and reached only to her knees, she still needed leggings, wrist coverings and a headscarf to avoid scratches and splinters.

"Did you get a whiff of that garbage pile outside? What a stench!" Mari exclaimed, her patchy brows shooting up.

"Uh, huh! It's bad."

"I told the market boss to have it hauled off twice a day, but he's too cheap. 'Only at night!' That's what he said," Mari complained.

Wrinkling up her nose, Aki whispered, "It's disgusting!"

After twisting her mouth to the side for a second, Mari asked, "Say, did you hear?"

"No, what?" answered Aki, now dabbing at the back of her neck with the handkerchief.

"Someone attacked the governor yesterday at the festival," replied Mari. "It was at the end of the float procession."

Aki, who had been tucking the handkerchief back under her sash, stopped and said, "What?"

"Yesterday, on Teramachi Avenue, a fellow threw a scroll at the governor."

"No!"

"Uh, huh. And that's not all," stated Mari. "Later in the day, someone posted notes on announcement boards saying imperial loyalists are rising up against the shōgun."

"What? Where?"

"Outside Gion Shrine. Those announcements were meant for the eyes of the Heavenly king sitting in his sacred palanquin. He'd see them when he was being carried back to the shrine."

"Really!" Aki cocked her head, considering the message boards.

"I don't know what the world's coming to," Mari lamented.

"Who would do such a thing?" Aki asked.

"No one knows. Not yet, anyway. But I bet it was Shining Blade."

"Shining Blade?"

"Uh, huh. He's tricky."

Remembering something Mari had told her—that Shining Blade was spotted near the market—Aki inquired, "Has he been seen around *here* lately?"

"No. Not that I've heard. But you never know with a scoundrel like that."

Aki pressed her lips together.

Just then a customer walked up to Mari's stall and began examining the sweet potatoes. Mari turned back to Aki, saying, "I got work to do, Little Aki. First, let me get you those provisions for the convent."

Mari bent over and pulled out a bundle wrapped in fabric. Setting the bundle on the counter and pushing it toward Aki, Mari grimaced with a warning. "Watch out, young miss. You can't be too careful on those mountain trails."

"I'll be careful," Aki replied, taking the bundle and leaving the market.

*　　*　　*

What was written in that scroll thrown at the governor? Aki wondered, crouching in her yard.

Aki had returned home, greeted her mother and started her chores. By late afternoon, she had completed preparations for her morning deliveries, retrieving enough kindling from a nearby slope to create three bundles of firewood. She had bound the sticks and twigs together and stacked the bundles in the yard.

Now, Aki was busy with another task she'd promised her mother she'd do, cleaning out the wide-mouthed jar used for storing rapeseed oil. With an old rag, she wiped down the insides, catching the aroma of the oil—pungent, roasted and slightly sulfurous. Once she was finished scrubbing the interior, she washed the exterior of the jar, admiring the natural glaze dripping down the body. She set the thick, sturdy pot upside down to dry on a square of hemp fabric and ran her index finger along the raised wave pattern incised on the pot's shoulder.

After wringing out the cleaning cloth, Aki washed her hands in a bucket of clean water outside the door of her hut. Nearby in the yard, Natsu had started preparing dinner, cutting the stems off spinach leaves on the outdoor chopping block. Aki went to join her.

"Mom—" Aki hesitated. "Have you heard anything about Shining Blade?"

"The dorobō?" asked Natsu. "They say he's causing trouble again."

"Granny Mari told me he might be the one who threw something at the governor yesterday. Is that true?"

"Uh, huh," Natsu murmured. "What an unfortunate incident! Luckily, the governor wasn't injured."

"Mom—" Aki hesitated again before going on. "Was Shining Blade spotted near here?"

Natsu turned her head away. She seemed to be staring at something across their yard, but when Aki looked, there was nothing at the spot but trees and shrubs. At last, Natsu replied calmly, "I overheard someone say that a thief showed up near Yamabana Market. No need to worry, though."

"Really?"

Natsu nodded, adding, "Still, you have to be cautious when you're out and about, Aki."

"Yes, I'm careful." Aki stopped, not sure what to say next. She couldn't read her mother's expression.

"Aki, would you go check the water on the stove?"

"Sure." Aki headed toward the kitchen, thinking she'd better give up on her questions for now. She sensed her mother didn't want to talk about Shining Blade.

Aki and Natsu prepared dinner together in silence. When it was ready, they sat down at the table and ate quietly. All Natsu said throughout the meal was, "Hot today, huh?"

Before long, they were done with dinner and clearing the table. Natsu went to the kitchen, and Aki stepped outside to wash the bowls and the pots. When she was finished, she joined her mother inside at the hearth to sit and drink tea. Natsu lit two small oil lamps.

Then as Natsu's solemn mood changed, she smiled playfully. She reached out and pulled on the edge of Aki's sleeve. "Hey, maybe this is a good night for a scary story. Like my mother used to say, scary stories make shivers run down your spine."

Aki nodded, suggesting, "How about a yōkai tale?"

"Sure. Let's see. Which tale haven't you heard yet, Aki? How about the gape-mouthed ghost?" Natsu smiled. "Have I told you that one?"

"No. Not yet."

As Natsu furrowed her brow in concentration, light from the pair of oil lamps flickered across her face. Relaxing, she leaned back and began. "Long, long ago, there was a young woman named Akiko who was brave and strong—like you, Aki."

"Ha!" Aki replied with a laugh.

Natsu continued. "One night, as Akiko was returning home from town, she decided to take a break and rest near a deserted riverbank. She stopped and sat on a fallen tree trunk in the moonlight. Akiko closed her eyes, listening to the gurgling of the stream behind her. All of a sudden, our heroine felt something touching her leg. It was cold and stiff. She reached out and grabbed it, realizing it was the end of a piece of rope."

"Rope?" Aki asked, amused. "Did the rope just come to life?"

"No!" Natsu replied, leaning toward Aki with her eyebrows raised. "What Akiko was holding was the rope that a terrible fellow had used to tie up a poor old widow and steal her Buddha statue. The widow had died like that, all tied up. That made the man a murderer."

"So, did he throw the rope at Akiko?" Aki asked.

"No, now wait. Let me finish the story," Natsu scolded her daughter in good humor. "Akiko didn't yet know about that man. One minute, our heroine was sitting still, and the next she was jumping up with a rope in her hands. She rushed to the river and was about to throw it in the water, when suddenly a fellow with disheveled hair appeared. He had a sickly complexion and an ugly sneer. He just stood there, blocking her way."

Aki pulled back her chin, thinking of the awful toothless fellow who had accosted her near the Yamabana Market several days earlier. She groaned, "Ach! This story's getting scary! What happened next?"

Natsu went on. "Akiko got angry at the fellow and asked him why he was out at night tricking innocent passersby."

"Good question!"

"And guess what happened next?" Natsu paused dramatically.

Her eyes wide, Aki asked, "What?"

"That fellow opened his terrible mouth and moaned, 'I'm a ghost. I was killed while trying to rob an elderly widow. Now, do as I say'." Natsu's voice had changed to a low rumble as she spoke the words of the ghost.

"The ghost started giving orders?" Aki asked.

Natsu smiled and went on, "Our heroine shook her head, placed her hands on her hips and declared, 'You're a monster. I do not obey monsters.'"

Aki laughed. "Ha! Me either!"

"Wait, Aki. With that, the fellow's eyes became large like washbasins, and his mouth became a gaping hole. He had transformed into a hideous yōkai." Natsu opened her eyes as wide as they would go and unhinged her jaw, reaching toward Aki with her hands dangling in front of her. Then she stopped, and her calm expression returned. She continued, "Our heroine stood up tall and declared, 'I will not be frightened.'"

"I don't know," Aki mumbled. "Maybe she should be a *little* scared."

"No, because our heroine knew that people who die while committing crimes become hungry ghosts. They turn into tortured souls who try to trick the living into dying the same way they did. Those hungry ghosts believe that's the only way their spirits will be free from torment. But our brave, young Aki—Woops! I meant to say Akiko—knew nothing would happen to her if she just remained composed."

"Oh!" Aki paused. "So, what happened next?"

"The ghost disappeared, and Akiko returned home safely."

"Huh? That's the end?"

"Yes. The end," answered Natsu, smiling.

Aki brought her palms together, making a soft clap. "Good story!"

Pulling on her daughter's sleeve again, Natsu remarked, "Sometimes tales of the supernatural serve a purpose. Right? You're not feeling the day's heat any more. Are you, Aki?"

"No. I'm shivering. Ha!" Aki laughed.

"Good!" Natsu sat back and said with a yawn, "Let's get ready for bed."

Aki murmured her agreement, and the two made their way to the kitchen. After helping clean up, Aki went to visit the outhouse, and, upon making a hasty return, she bolted the door behind her. Noticing that her mother was arranging the mosquito nets around their bedding, Aki started in, saying, "Mom—"

Natsu interrupted. "It's late, Aki, and I'm tired. Let's get some sleep."

Aki dropped her head and crawled into bed. She watched as her mother extinguished the oil lamps and settled under her own thin blanket. Soon Aki closed her eyes. She didn't fall asleep right away, however.

Mom should stop being so protective, Aki thought. She clearly doesn't want to tell me about Shining Blade. Instead, she invents a story about a brave young woman and a cruel thief who becomes a ghost. Oh, well. I'll find out about Shining Blade, one way or another.

Her thoughts spinning like a top, Aki remained awake in the dark for over an hour. Finally, her mind slowed, and she fell asleep.

PART 4

BACKGROUND: COURT
AND ARISTOCRATS

Loyal Reader, in case you're beginning to conceive of 1654 Kyoto as a city dominated by warriors and townspeople, let me remind you of another group, the hereditary imperial elite. In days of old—when people called Japan a sacred land—it was an emperor who occupied the place of honor in Kyoto. People said the emperor was a divine intermediary showering blessings on the realm. Yet, while emperors had wielded supreme power during early eras, by 1654, the monarch was no longer in charge of military or governmental affairs. Those functions now fell squarely on shogunal shoulders.

Still highly respected—no, revered—the emperor preserved traditional scholarship, conferred sought-after court titles and set standards for cultural accomplishment. From far off in Edo, the Tokugawa called upon the monarch to preserve an imperial heritage of elite aristocratic culture. The emperor, ensconced in his palace at the heart of Kyoto, willingly complied. But when the Tokugawa forbad the emperor from engaging in political activity, the palace wasn't so happy. This was the balance they eventually struck—the emperor could depend on Tokugawa generosity if he ensured preservation of Tokugawa rule by designating the shogunal heir as his successor. Yet, the peace between emperors and shōguns was not an easy one.

The patriarch of the imperial family in 1654 was former Emperor GoMizunoo, who had retired over two decades earlier but who had lived on, surviving the tenure of four Tokugawa shōguns. GoMizunoo's position was unenviable. He was relentlessly manipulated by the Tokugawa, who even coerced him into marrying the second shōgun's daughter, Tōfukumon'in, no doubt intending for a son of this union to take the throne, such that the Tokugawa bloodline would be passed down to both the shōgun in Edo and the emperor in Kyoto. However, that was not to be because no such son survived to become emperor.

Sitting on the throne in 1654 was Emperor GoKōmyō, the son of GoMizunoo and an aristocratic lady. GoKōmyō faced a number of challenges with Tokugawa authorities, but he also enjoyed the luxuries of court life, competing in poetry contests, sponsoring rounds of games and inspecting treasured collectibles. In this, he resembled an older relative, Prince Hachijō Toshitada, one of the leading aficionados of Kyoto. At this point, Toshitada was busy expanding upon his father's Katsura Villa, turning the rural grounds into a stunning estate where he hosted an impressive range of luminaries.

Not all members of the imperial family gave themselves over to pleasurable diversions. There were those who performed the requisite and complex court rituals, as well as those who dedicated themselves to religious pursuits, becoming monks, nuns, priests and priestesses. These devotees lived in or near Kyoto at imperial temples, convents and shrines. While some such establishments served as extensions of the court, others differed markedly, including Enshōji. A Rinzai Zen convent, Enshōji was established and overseen by Abbess Bunchi, the eldest daughter of the retired emperor. Located in the scenic northeastern foothills of Kyoto, Enshōji was a strict religious community of nuns. In fact, one of the nuns at Enshōji, Sister Bunkai, plays a central role in our story.

A GIFT FOR THE NUN

"WHAT'S THIS, AKI? SHALL I OPEN IT?" ASKED BUNKAI.

"Please do." Aki nodded. A few minutes earlier, she had arrived for a lesson at the imperial convent of Enshōji. Entering the study of the Ryokuin'an subtemple, she had found it empty. After setting her gift for Bunkai on the nun's desk, she'd gone and taken a seat at her own desk, waiting for her teacher to return. It wasn't long before the door had opened and Bunkai had joined her.

Now the nun picked up the gift, removed the saffron-colored wrapping paper and, seeing what was inside, she smiled. "How perfect, Aki! I've been wanting a wind chime for the veranda."

"I thought you'd like that color, Sister Bunkai."

"I do. This rich brown is my favorite. It's mellow."

"Uh, huh. Mellow. That's a good word for it."

"And the rabbit is charming. It's so skillfully drawn. Thank you, Aki." The nun looked up, clearly happy. Then, still holding the chime in one cupped hand, she remarked, "By the way, Prince Toshitada and the Manshuin abbot send their greetings."

"Oh!" Aki's eyes widened.

Bunkai carefully set down the chime and shifted on her cushion. She pointed at a scroll unrolled on Aki's desk and said, "Are you ready to get started?"

"Uh, huh," Aki replied, leaning over her desktop and examining the document there. She recognized it as a series of poems written in a refined script. One poem described cherry blossoms in spring, and another spoke of the moon in autumn. After scrutinizing the poems, Aki prepared her ink and began writing. It wasn't long, though, before she was fidgeting with her writing box.

Glancing up from a note she'd been writing, Bunkai asked, "Is something wrong, Aki?"

"Sister Bunkai, would you tell me more about Prince Toshitada and the Manshuin abbot?"

"Certainly. Where should I start?"

"Well—" Aki hesitated for a moment. "What were the prince and the abbot talking about when I heard them that time at the Manshuin entrance?"

Instead of answering, the nun lifted her chin and looked out into the garden.

Aki followed Bunkai's gaze. The garden looks fresh and orderly, Aki said to herself. The convent manservant must have clipped the bushes and raked the gravel recently. There's nothing unusual out there, though. Sister Bunkai must be thinking about something private.

Aki waited quietly and eventually Bunkai's focus returned to her desk. That's when Aki jumped back in with her questions. "Sister Bunkai, why are Prince Toshitada and the Manshuin abbot so upset with the shōgun? I don't understand why the shōgun needs to cause the emperor trouble, forcing him to marry his granddaughter. And why did the shōgun deny the emperor permission to train with a sword?"

"Aki, one question at a time!" responded Bunkai, her hands shooting up, palms facing her student. After taking a deep breath and exhaling slowly, the nun began to explain. "Since you inquired about the reverend mother's relatives, let's start with the poems I selected for your lesson today. They were written by the father of Prince Toshitada and the Manshuin abbot."

"Their father?"

"Yes. He was the former Prince Toshihito. His calligraphy is exceptional. Don't you think?"

Aki nodded. "What was he like, Sister Bunkai?"

"My mother saw the former prince often when she was young and remembers him vividly. He was an accomplished man of culture. He often attended gatherings to compose poetry, and he appreciated the art of Tea ceremony. He dedicated himself to sophisticated pastimes, just as his sons do today. The former prince was a remarkable person, but he was caught up in a difficult situation. He was adopted by the most powerful warlord in the realm—the Taikō."

"Oh! He was adopted by the Taikō!"

"Yes. That was more than sixty years ago."

"So, court families allow their sons to be adopted like samurai families?"

"They do, Aki. But let me resume. Prince Toshihito was twelve years old when the Taikō adopted him. Several years later, the Taikō's concubine gave birth to a boy. With a son of his own, the Taikō annulled the adoption of Prince

Toshihito. The warlord compensated Toshihito by granting him permission to establish a new princely line called the Hachijō. Aki, are you following all this?"

"Uh, huh." Aki bobbed her head and leaned forward resting her chin in one palm.

Bunkai continued. "The Taikō also gave Prince Toshihito land at Katsura. Toshihito built a modest residence surrounded by melon fields there. When Toshihito died, his eldest son, our Prince Toshitada, inherited the land, but it had been sitting untended for years. Toshitada is now refurbishing the Katsura estate. He's decided to add Tea arbors and improve the landscaped grounds."

Bunkai continued. "And I'm sure the new grounds of Manshuin near here will be as wonderful as Prince Toshitada's estate at Katsura. Courtiers and ladies will be invited to visit the temple to enjoy the gorgeous scenery and stroll through the gardens. They'll view fine paintings, play the shell matching game and enjoy other pastimes."

In her mind's eye, Aki pictured refined gentlemen and lovely ladies arriving in lacquered palanquins and passing under a majestic gate at the Manshuin main entrance.

Bunkai tucked her chin and waited for her student to regain her focus.

Realizing the nun was watching her, Aki mumbled, "Please go on, Sister Bunkai."

"No doubt the Manshuin abbot will become renowned as a host. Of the two of them, though, I suspect it's Prince Toshitada that people will be talking about for decades to come. He's quite a lively character. But enough of that." Bunkai moved to stand, explaining, "I need to leave again to attend to matters in the kitchen. Continue working on your transcription, Aki. I'll be back in a short while."

"Yes, Sister Bunkai."

Bunkai rose up and moved toward the door. Before opening it, she turned back and gave Aki a challenge. "Let's see how well you can imitate the former prince's calligraphy."

Aki smiled and picked up her brush, resuming her work with new enthusiasm.

"Deputy Inspector Tanaka, tell me again what happened that morning," ordered Magistrate Gomi, his voice even hoarser than usual.

"Yes, your excellency," replied Tanaka, understanding that Gomi was asking him to review the incident at the closing procession of the Gion Festival. Tanaka was back at Second Street Encampment, reporting to the magistrate. Keeping his gaze fixed downward on the tatami, Tanaka proceeded to recount basics he had already included in written reports.

Gomi listened carefully to Tanaka's account and then, squaring his shoulders, he set his palms on his desktop and stated, "In one of your reports, you claim to have witnessed a hand emerge from inside the Halberd float. Correct?"

"That is correct, sir."

The magistrate continued. "That hand threw out one of the two scrolls?"

"Yes, sir."

"Tanaka, you're confident the perpetrators had crawled inside the lower part of the float and were hiding there behind the curtains?"

"Yes, sir."

"Hmm." After pulling on one earlobe for a moment, Gomi lifted his chin and said, "Tell me more."

"Behind the curtain at the interior of the wheeled floats, there's a wooden scaffolding, sir. It's mostly open space. It would have provided room for several men to hide."

"Yes. That's plausible," Gomi mumbled, speaking more to himself than to the deputy inspector. After coughing, he went on to say, "But all you saw was a hand throwing a scroll. Correct? No face?"

"That is correct, sir. I didn't catch a face or any identifying features. As I wrote in my report, I presume there were two people hiding there. A second person must have been behind the curtain on the opposite side of the float. That person must have thrown the scroll toward Governor Itakura in the viewing gallery."

"Yes, I see. Your agents chased after the float and—" Gomi held off, allowing Tanaka to explain his hypothesis.

"Yes, sir. The two agents who followed the Halberd float found it on Fourth Street, moving toward Karasuma Avenue. Once it came to a stop, the agents checked inside the float, under the curtains, and found no one. There was nothing unusual in the interior."

"And the agents spoke with leaders of the float?"

"Yes, sir. When the agents explained what had happened, the two float leaders expressed complete surprise. The agents were introduced to the pullers and riders, who also claimed ignorance of the incident. The agents verified that everyone associated with the Halberd float resides on the block that sponsored the float. They are well known to one another. The agents took down their names, as well as names of the musicians who had been sitting on the upper story of the float with the three boys. They all said they'd encountered no suspicious individuals attempting to gain access to the float."

"Hmm," Gomi muttered, as he sat back thinking.

Tanaka continued. "Later, before the float was dismantled, I inspected it. As I wrote in my report, sir, I found nothing out of the ordinary."

"I suppose the perpetrators could have slipped out from under the curtain soon after throwing the two scrolls. With the crowds and the clamor, they could easily have escaped undetected before your agents got there."

"Agreed, sir."

"Tanaka, you still believe the individual responsible for the scrolls is the rōnin Ishida Kurōbei?"

"Yes. I do, sir."

Pausing, Gomi pulled on his earlobe. Then he asked, "What more have you learned about Ishida Kurōbei?"

"Very little, sir. Rumor has it he's a disgruntled rōnin. He's seeking revenge for alleged affronts."

"What about the two announcement boards placed outside Gion Shrine?"

"Sir, I presume Kurōbei ordered his men to erect those boards. He was aware our guards and agents would be stationed along the route of the sacred palanquins and not at the shrine."

Scowling, Gomi declared, "The posting of those boards is unfortunate. Throwing scrolls at the governor is bad enough, but the postings are even worse—due to their public nature. It suggests that civilians can threaten Edo authorities with no consequences. This all points to something truly disturbing. I fear these rōnin may be planning an uprising in Kyoto."

"Ah!" Tanaka dipped his head, sucking in his breath.

"Deputy inspector, you say you tracked a suspicious man to First Street Temple district three days ago. You think it was Kurōbei?"

"I do, sir. Several witnesses identified him, accurately giving his age and height, as well as the prominent, jagged scar outside his left eye."

"I see." Gomi sat back, coughing again. Then, after moving his lower jaw back and forth several times, he said, "Tell me once more, Tanaka, when did you first hear of Ishida Kurōbei?"

"About five weeks ago, sir. I first heard his name in association with several robberies downtown. Victims and witnesses accused him of committing those crimes."

"Did Kurōbei act alone in those instances?" Gomi queried.

"Apparently, he did, sir."

"However, he now seems to be working with others?"

"Yes. That is my impression, sir."

"How many men do you think Kurōbei has working with him?"

"Perhaps ten or eleven, sir."

"Hmm. So, now he's directing the criminal activities of a crew." Gomi shook his head. "What about Kurōbei's background?"

"Sir, several witnesses claimed he spoke in a dialect—"

"Which dialect?"

"One witness suggested it was the Tanba vernacular, sir."

Gomi blinked hard. Other than that, he remained still for a long moment, until he adjusted his position and said, "Tanaka, from this point forward, when you interview witnesses, be sure to ask whether Kurōbei speaks in a recognizable manner."

"Yes, sir."

Scratching his chin, Gomi grew quiet again. At last, he spoke up, asking, "Any idea what Kurōbei might be planning next, Tanaka?"

"Sir, I've received no specific intelligence on the matter. However, Kurōbei's actions have become increasingly provocative. As you said, the announcement boards posted outside Gion Shrine publicly condemned the shogunal government. Given what he has communicated, it seems likely Kurōbei is planning a bigger and more inflammatory assault, perhaps on top Edo officials in Kyoto."

Grimacing, Gomi remarked, "I concur with your assessment, deputy inspector. This man Kurōbei must be apprehended."

"Understood, sir."

Gomi adjusted his posture and concluded the meeting. "That is all for now. Let me know of any developments."

"Yes, sir." Tanaka bowed deeply, stood and left the room.

As he walked across the grounds of Second Street Encampment, Tanaka noticed that winds had picked up and clouds were moving in from the west. Although the change was a welcome relief from the sweltering conditions earlier in the afternoon, the sky foretold an approaching storm. Picking up his pace, Tanaka headed directly to his study, anticipating that several agents were waiting for him there.

"Aki, I discovered who those two men were—the ones you overheard a while back," stated Bunkai.

In the middle of copying a poem, Aki lifted the tip of her brush from the paper in front of her and asked, "Who were they, Sister Bunkai?"

The nun had just returned to her desk in the Ryokuin'an study, after running a quick errand. Suppressing a smile, she whispered, "One was the abbot of Manshuin. And you're about to meet him."

"The Manshuin abbot?"

"Yes. He'll be here any minute now. We are honored to have him and—" Bunkai held off.

Footsteps on the stairs to the veranda were accompanied by the rustling of fabric. A man's voice called out a greeting. "Hello, Sister Bunkai."

"Please come in, your reverence," Bunkai responded, standing and moving toward the doorway.

Aki turned and bent at the waist in a deep bow, pressing her palms flat in front of her on the tatami mats. She heard the door slide open and a second voice join in.

"Good morning!" the second speaker said, his tone deep and velvety.

Aki lifted her head slightly, catching a glimpse of two pairs of feet in white tabi socks. She lowered her head again, her brow nearly touching the tatami. She remained in that position while Bunkai spoke to the visitors.

"Won't you take a seat?" Bunkai said politely as she closed the door and gestured toward two cushions, inviting her guests to sit.

The gentlemen lowered themselves onto their cushions, tucking their silk robes under their shins. Bunkai was last to sit. Aki didn't see any of that, though, as her head was still lowered. She picked up scents of clove, orange and aloeswood that had been used to perfume the men's garments.

When she finally looked up, Aki recognized the visitors immediately. They were the gentlemen she had encountered outside the Manshuin grounds weeks earlier. One was rather diminutive with a shaved head. The other seemed a bit older and had two hands lifted at his chest, holding a small box.

Eyes wide, Aki looked over at Bunkai. The nun ignored her glance.

Once everyone was settled, the gentleman with the shaved head turned to the nun. Aki had already identified him as Reverend Ryōshō, the Manshuin abbot. He wore the same monastic garments Aki had seen him in previously. Over a crisp undecorated robe of white silk, he had on a loose jacket of transparent black gauze.

The Manshuin abbot straightened his collar and started in, saying, "Please excuse our unannounced appearance, Sister Bunkai. My brother and I just learned that Miss Aki was here with you today, and we asked to come meet her. The Enshōji abbess approved, so here we are!"

"Wonderful!" Bunkai replied.

Aki noticed the second guest smiling mischievously at her. She guessed it was the Manshuin abbot's older brother, Prince Hachijō Toshitada. The prince set down the little box he had carried in.

Bunkai gestured toward Aki, saying, "Let me introduce my student. This is Aki."

"Ah! Miss Aki," the prince replied, exuding a refined sense of ease. His dark eyes gleamed.

Aki lowered her head and responded softly, her voice shaky. "I am deeply honored, your excellencies."

The nun turned to her student. "Aki, this is Prince Hachijō Toshitada and his younger brother, the Manshuin abbot."

"Your excellencies," Aki repeated in a whisper. She forgot to bow again.

"Nice to make your acquaintance, Miss Aki," the prince remarked.

Hearing the prince's cheerful greeting, Aki relaxed a bit and bowed again.

With swift, deliberate movements, the prince arranged the sleeves of his sumptuous robe, woven with a diamond pattern and dyed sky blue. Then he gently pushed toward Bunkai the little box, saying, "It's nothing much, but I hope you and Miss Aki will enjoy these candies from my estate."

Aki noticed that Toshitada's manner was formal but tranquil at the same time.

"For us, your excellency?" Bunkai asked with a tilt of her head.

"Yes."

"What a kind gesture, Prince Toshitada!" Bunkai dipped her head in thanks. "Everyone loves the sweets sold by women near your estate in Katsura."

"Well, I offered them to the Enshōji abbess, but she requested I bring them to you, Sister Bunkai."

"Ah!"

Aki watched as Bunkai extended her two hands, placed her fingertips on opposite sides of the box and slid it to her side. Aki had rarely seen Bunkai adopt such refined etiquette.

The prince directed his attention to the view of the garden out the door to the right. He exclaimed, "Now, that is a perfect design!"

"Indeed," the Manshuin abbot agreed. "The seasonal garden here is an elegant distillation of nature. It is the result of superb planning."

"Reverend, your words are much too generous," Bunkai answered modestly. "That reminds me—the hydrangea started blooming in town."

"Ha!" the prince laughed. "Sister Bunkai, you changed the subject. Do you find compliments as uncomfortable as the Enshōji abbess does? The abbess is ever alert to the merest hint of arrogance."

"No, no," replied Bunkai, waving her hand as if to disperse smoke wafting up before her.

Stepping in to save the nun from embarrassment, the Manshuin abbot remarked, "I also noticed the summer bushes blooming in town."

With that, the prince, the abbot and Bunkai launched into a discussion of hydrangeas. Listening silently, Aki took the opportunity to examine the visitors.

The prince was immaculately groomed, his jet-black hair combed back and set in place. Thanks to a light application of white powder, his face looked perfectly soft and smooth. Wispy sideburns extended down his jawline toward his strong chin. And his elegantly arched eyebrows complemented his aquiline nose.

The abbot, on the other hand, had a squat nose, a broad forehead and thinning brows. Dark stubble covered his head, and the hint of a beard set off his wide, relaxed mouth. His expression was benevolent.

Despite their differences, the brothers shared a certain glimmer in their eyes and a rich, mellow quality to their voices.

Feeling Bunkai nudge her elbow, Aki suddenly awoke to the fact she had been staring at the prince and the abbot with her mouth agape.

Bunkai smiled and said to the others, "You must forgive Aki. This is quite extraordinary for her."

Realizing that the two brothers were struggling to hold back their amusement, Aki dropped her head and stared into her own lap. Her cheeks felt hot.

The Manshuin abbot returned to the previous subject, squinting and remarking, "Your garden does capture the very best of nature, Sister Bunkai."

"This is but a poor mountain hermitage, sir," the nun responded with a shake of her head. "I beg your indulgence—"

"No, no," replied the Manshuin abbot. "Don't disparage your blessed residence, Sister Bunkai. We're very fond of this spot. The views from up here are marvelous. My eyesight might be poor, but I can still enjoy beautiful scenery."

"Indeed!" Beaming, Toshitada threw out his arms, causing his long silken sleeves to flutter. "The Enshōji abbess was kind enough to show me around last time I visited. The spot up the hill provides such expansive vistas. I was amazed to see the rivers and forests stretching out across the northern foothills."

"Thank you, your excellency," responded Bunkai, lowering her head and bringing her palms together in a gesture of prayer.

As Toshitada shot a dazzling smile at his companions, Aki felt her eyes opening in wonderment. The prince had captivated her.

Now Toshitada reached into one of his sleeves and pulled out a folding fan. Snapping the fan open with a flick of his wrist, he began slowly sweeping it in front of his face. After a moment, he stopped and rested the fan on his right knee.

Aki examined the fan. The front face was painted in rich mineral colors with a scene of pine trees on a shoreline buffeted by waves. A sprinkling of gold dust suggested sea spray. That's so refreshing, Aki thought. Perfect for a sultry day like this.

"Sister Bunkai, should we not get down to business?" Toshitada inquired. "I wonder whether your promising student, Miss Aki, would be willing to tell us a little about herself? I hear she's a scholar-in-training."

All eyes turned to Aki, sitting mute and immobile. What did the prince expect her to say?

Bunkai came to her student's rescue. "Your excellencies, let me tell you a few things about Aki. She lives up the mountain from here with her mother, a Shirakawa flower seller. A few years ago, I began teaching Aki to read and write. Aki has been attending lessons here once a week. She has advanced rapidly and now copies sutras and poems, and at times she joins us for Buddhist chanting and prayers. She can even recite scripture from memory."

Aki remained silent.

Bunkai continued. "Aki's mother trained her to gather kindling on the mountain slopes and to carry it into town. Six days a week, my student gets up early and goes into town with bundles of kindling on her head. Aki is robust and punctual. Each day, she delivers a bundle to three different clients. Aki has eighteen clients all together. I selected them myself. They include monastic establishments and aristocratic households, places where your siblings and cousins live."

The prince lifted an eyebrow. "Sister Bunkai, are you saying the young lady is already delivering firewood to the locations that concern us?"

"Yes, sir."

"Does that include the convents of Hōkyōji and Jissōin, the temple of Shōgōin and the Nagataniden residence?"

"Yes, sir."

"Does it include estates of the Ichijō, the Nijō and the Konoe?"

"It does, your excellency."

The prince and the abbot tipped their heads in unison, pleased to hear about Aki's clients.

"Then the groundwork has been laid," the prince pronounced with evident satisfaction.

"Yes, your excellency. It has," Bunkai agreed. "And Aki has already started delivering letters in her kindling bundles to your relatives. Once the reverend mother has given me her letters, I roll them up and slip them into a hollow section of bamboo. Then I hide them in Aki's kindling bundles. Each morning she delivers three letters and brings others back to me in the afternoon."

After staring at Aki for a moment, the prince nodded. "This young lady is perfect—unassuming and simple in her presentation."

Squinting at Aki, the Manshuin abbot agreed. "Yes, she is."

"By the way—" Bunkai hesitated. "I believe my student recognizes the two of you."

Aki felt her jaw drop slightly.

Prince Toshitada responded with a little smile, mumbling, "Is that so?" He turned to his brother and repeated, "Miss Aki is already familiar with us!"

Aki squirmed, expecting to be reprimanded for having listened in on a private conversation between the prince and the abbot.

"Ha, ha!" Toshitada laughed, flashing his eyes at Aki. "We already know that you overheard me speaking with my brother, Miss Aki. Sister Bunkai told us you were hiding outside the Manshuin gate. Not to worry. It's just as well."

"Yes," the Manshuin abbot concurred. "There's no reason you should worry about having listened in on us, Miss Aki."

"Oh! Thank goodness!" Aki let out a sharp breath.

"But don't tell strangers what we were discussing!" the prince declared, his tone cautionary.

"No!" Aki answered. "I won't, your excellency."

The prince furrowed his brow and continued. "You must be careful, Miss Aki. Kyoto is teeming with criminals. Don't let people's appearance fool you. Trouble lies in wait."

"Of course, sir." Aki pressed her lips together.

The prince went on. "Let me clarify another thing, Miss Aki. You must never reveal that you spoke with us. And *never* say you are serving as our messenger."

"Yes, sir."

"Furthermore, if you and I ever meet on a street in town, or even on a trail in these foothills, I will not greet you. For your own wellbeing, I will not admit to knowing you. Understood?"

"Yes, sir."

The Manshuin abbot was next to warn Aki, but in a gentler manner. "Unfortunately, Miss Aki, that applies to me, as well. In public, I will behave as if I never met you. It might seem unfair, but it's for your own safety. Oh! Also, try to avoid the impulse to uncover things on your own."

"Yes, sir."

The abbot wasn't done yet. "You must be vigilant, Miss Aki, and you must not arouse suspicion. Your work will be dangerous. The letters you carry are highly confidential."

"I understand." Aki glanced at Bunkai.

Without returning the look, Bunkai shook her head. "I do regret involving Aki in our affairs. She's an innocent young woman. But I suppose there's no other way. Shigata ga arimasen."

The Manshuin abbot leaned toward the nun, saying, "Do not worry, Sister Bunkai. We will do everything we can to protect Miss Aki."

"Yes, we will." Toshitada gave a single firm nod. Lifting one hand to cover his mouth, he coughed discreetly and added, "But now it's time for us to depart."

With that, the prince and the abbot said their farewells and stood to leave. As Bunkai ushered them to the door, the prince touched the nun's elbow and remarked, "Sister Bunkai, I suppose you've heard—an outlaw rōnin is on the loose. He has killed several people."

"Yes, I was warned," Bunkai replied.

"Be on your guard—"

Aki couldn't make out Toshitada's next words, uttered while stepping over the threshold and onto the veranda. As he and his brother turned back to bow, the nun and her student, already bent forward, lowered their heads even deeper. Once the prince and the abbot had descended the stairs and were crossing the courtyard, Bunkai slid the door closed.

The nun turned to Aki, saying, "The morning has slipped by so quickly. It must be time for me to join others in the prayer hall. We should hurry and clean up."

Aki returned to her desk, placed her writing utensils in their box and straightened the pile of papers containing her transcriptions. She expressed her appreciation for the opportunity to meet the prince and the abbot. Then she stood and left the Ryokuin'an.

On her way home, Aki reflected on the unusual comments made by Prince Toshitada and the Manshuin abbot. The prince is charming, she mused. And fascinating.

Aki felt like skipping, but instead she slowed, seeing the majestic cedar tree ahead. She stopped to offer a prayer. Then, picking up her pace, she continued up the trail, anxious to tell her mother about meeting the prince and the abbot.

It's so hot and humid! Aki sighed.

For Aki, the sweltering weather was making deliveries a challenge, just as on the day before. Now approaching the Konoe residence for her last drop-off, she was beginning to feel faint. Aki tried taking her mind off her discomfort by thinking about news she might learn from the Konoe kitchen maid.

Sumi might have a secret or two! Aki said to herself. On the other hand, maybe she'll start babbling about Shining Blade. I hope she doesn't end up getting all prickly again.

As Aki turned down the alley that led to the Konoe kitchen, she spotted Sumi facing the opposite direction and wiping her hands on her apron. Aki noticed how frail the young maid seemed. When Sumi turned, Aki caught sight of the maid's pouty face.

Sumi came running, grabbed Aki's elbow and led her away from the gate. In a low voice, she said, "Sister Aki, you didn't *tell* anyone. Did you?"

"About what?" Aki asked teasingly.

Failing to catch on, Sumi whispered, "About me feeding the dogs."

"About what? See—I already forgot. What was it again?" Aki looked Sumi in the eye.

Sumi's jaw dropped as she frowned.

"No, Sister Sumi. I didn't say anything," Aki clarified to reassure the maid. Meanwhile, she removed the kindling from her head, set it at her feet and shrugged her shoulders to loosen her tight muscles.

"Good!" Sumi grinned.

Noticing that Sumi was missing one of her lower cuspids, Aki asked, "How did you lose your tooth, Sister Sumi?"

"In a fight."

"Oh!" Aki stopped, thinking she probably shouldn't ask for details.

"Anyway, thanks for not saying anything about the dogs, Sister Aki. I don't know why the master chef has to be so strict. He's really mean, and his eyes are weird. I call him the Cross-Eyed Monster. He, he!"

By reflex, Aki pulled back her chin, surprised by Sumi's insolence.

"What difference does it make if I feed the dogs a few scraps? No one else is eating the leftovers. They'd be wasted."

"Hmm. Right, but—" Aki stopped, interrupted by the maid.

"All I'm doing is helping our fellow creatures," Sumi added defensively. "I think the merciful bodhisattva would approve. Praise be to the bodhisattva."

"Yes," Aki repeated in all seriousness. "Praise be to the bodhisattva. The bodhisattva eases the suffering of sentient beings."

As Sumi's ears perked up, she asked, "Are you a devotee of the bodhisattva, Sister Aki?"

"I am. My teacher taught me to pray to the bodhisattva of compassion."

"Who's your teacher?"

"Sister Bunkai at the convent of Enshōji in Shugakuin."

"Where's Shugakuin?"

"Not far from where I live. On the way up to Mount Hiei."

"What! You live up there?" Sumi pointed off toward the northeast.

"Yes. Why?"

"Your home is on that mountainside?" Sumi asked, incredulous. "Why do you live so far away?"

Peeved by Sumi's tone, Aki replied, "So I can easily gather kindling. That's why!"

"And you're pledging to become a nun?"

"No. But the convent is a special place. I respect the Enshōji abbess and Sister Bunkai. They're dedicated to Buddhist practice."

"What! I knew it! You're one of those holier-than-thou types!"

Aki winced, taken aback by Sumi's sarcastic comment. "What do you mean, Miss Sumi? You're the one who brought it up. You said, 'Praise be to the bodhisattva'."

Swatting at the air, Sumi replied, "That's just a phrase people use."

"What?"

"Well, I *do* pray to the bodhisattva now and then, when I need help." Sumi screwed up her face. "But I'm not smug about it. Not me!"

Again dismayed, Aki took a step back.

"How can you hang around with all those nuns?" Sumi asked.

"What are you talking about?"

"Nuns are as bad as monks," declared Sumi with a shake of her head.

Feeling offended, Aki replied, "I know a lot of nuns and monks who are fine people."

"Like who?" Sumi shot back.

"Like Sister Bunkai and Abbess Bunchi. And the Manshuin abbot. He's from the imperial family."

"Ha!" Sumi laughed out loud. "What's so great about them?"

Resisting an impulse to turn and walk away, Aki steadied her voice and went on. "The abbess and the abbot are both highly educated individuals. They are also very gifted. And the Manshuin abbot is building a wonderful temple."

"La-di-da. Look at Sister Aki—she's in love with a Buddhist monk. And he's from the emperor's family." Sumi lifted her nose in the air, pretending to be snobby aristocrat.

Aki had never heard anything as callous as this, even though she'd heard Shugakuin villagers mock highbrow people. She replied, "All I meant to say is that men and women can live in peace at a monastery or at a convent."

"Yeah, sure," Sumi scoffed. "Sounds boring. I prefer warriors and rōnin, like Shining Blade. They say he's tall and agile and—"

"Aren't you scared of him, Sister Sumi?"

Waving her hand dismissively, Sumi chortled, "Ha, ha! Not me! Not at all. I hope to meet him one day. I bet he's got a deep voice. And gorgeous eyes. I just know it."

"What?" Aki winced. "That man's a murderer. He killed a gate attendant and a clerk."

"Come on, Sister Aki. He's not so bad. People just talk."

"And for good reason. People are saying everyone is in danger. Even the emperor."

"I doubt it," Sumi shook her head. "The emperor's got teams of armed guards to protect him. I ought to know. I've worked in this neighborhood for seven years now."

"You have?"

"Yup. I've been around. I've seen a lot. And I've heard a lot, too. If it's secrets you want, Sister Aki, I got lots of them!"

"Do you know why the shōgun refused the emperor's request to train with a sword?"

"No!" Sumi glared at Aki. "How could I know about that? Stop asking stupid questions. You're just making fun of me, aren't you."

"No!" Aki demurred. "Sorry if that's what you thought, Miss Sumi."

"Well, I'll admit it. My parents were poor tenant farmers."

"I see," Aki muttered.

"Since I was a little girl, they told me I'd have to earn my own way. They asked my uncle to help me. He sells cooking oil, and he's got connections in the imperial kitchen. So, he found a place for me at the Ichijō residence. But I couldn't stay there. I had to move to the Iwakura residence. Then, not long after that, I had to move again. I ended up here in the Konoe kitchen." Sumi stopped and hung her head. After a few seconds, though, she looked up with a chuckle and asked, "Ha! Why'd your parents give you the name Aki?"

Less unnerved now by Sumi's unpredictability, Aki answered, "Because I was born in the autumn. How about you?"

"When I was a baby, my hair was so black it soaked up the sunlight like sumi ink. It's still really dark."

Aki glanced at Sumi's hair, which was tied up in a scarf. All Aki could see were a few dark strands tucked behind the maid's ears. So, she moved on to ask, "Have you got any news about Shining Blade, Sister Sumi?"

"Uh, huh. The police *still* haven't managed to track him down! I bet he's hiding in the forest. His life must be full of adventure."

"Hmm," Aki mumbled with a shake of her head. "I don't know."

"Oh! There's another thing you should know, Sister Aki. Shining Blade has been spotted in your part of town—at a place of worship in the Shugakuin neighborhood. Isn't that where your teacher's convent is located?"

"It is. Was he seen at a convent?"

"I don't know. I've never even been up there."

Aki rocked from her heels to her toes, rubbing the back of her neck.

Noticing Aki's anxious response, Sumi added, "But Shining Blade's days are numbered. Oh! That reminds me. I heard about some outlaw named Kurōbei. Lord Konoe was talking about him recently. He was speaking with Lord Ichijō. He said this guy Kurōbei is skilled with the sword.

Sounds fascinating, huh! According to Lord Ichijō, Kurōbei admires a great swordsman from the old days."

"Really? What's his name?"

"How should I know?" Sumi spat back, irritated yet again. "Anyway, that swordman was famous for having won duels against a whole crew of men in the district of First Street Temple."

"What? I pass through there almost every day."

"Well, if it was me, and I was passing through that district, I'd keep my eyes peeled for a tall, handsome man with two swords—Ishida Kurōbei, I mean. He might happen to walk by. Or maybe there're other good-looking men hanging around First Street Temple district."

Not this again! Sumi is plain man crazy, Aki thought.

Aki warned the maid, "I'd be watching my back, Sister Sumi."

"No! I can handle men," Sumi smirked.

Aki blinked hard. Then, deciding to change the subject, she asked, "So, what is Lord Konoe like?"

"Not very interesting. He's like *every* nobleman I've ever seen—shriveled up and stupid. They're so boring! Like I said, I used to serve in other kitchens near here." Sumi gestured toward estates at her right and left before eyeing Aki and waiting, as if daring Aki to inquire about something private.

"Well," Aki countered. "There's one nobleman who's *not* boring. He's just the opposite—Prince Toshitada."

"Prince Toshitada?"

"Uh, huh. He's the Manshuin abbot's brother. The prince excels at calligraphy and verse, and he's a dynamic, cultured gentleman."

Sumi put a hand on one hip and rolled her eyes, shaking her head. "Whatever you say, Sister Aki."

"He is!"

"Sure," Sumi replied. "And I suppose you met this Prince Toshitada?"

"Well—" Aki hesitated, remembering her promise to stay quiet. "No. I haven't."

Stopping abruptly, as if she'd heard someone nearby, Sumi leaned toward Aki and mumbled, "I got to get back to work. See you next time."

Aki nodded. "Alright. Bye!"

With that, Sumi ran back to the Konoe kitchen gate and disappeared.

"SIR, WE FOUND TWO WITNESSES!" THE WOLF WHISPERED. HE had arrived in a rush to report to Deputy Inspector Tanaka.

"Bring them here," ordered Tanaka.

The Wolf, who had on the tattered garments of a carpenter and a roughly woven bamboo hat, gave a firm nod and rushed off.

It was a scorching afternoon, and most people were hiding out in some shady spot. But in the First Street Temple district of northeastern Kyoto, a few pedestrians were still out and about. Among them were Tanaka and two of his undercover agents—The Wolf and The Crab—who had been conducting separate patrols for several hours, intending to catch the murderous thief Ishida Kurōbei. After meandering around outside the main market in the district, Tanaka had stopped across from a stall selling pinwheel toys. Dressed in disguise—wearing a dusty, old jacket with a square of pale cotton wrapped around his head, one end tucked under in front—the deputy inspector had been watching people come and go, hoping to lay eyes on Kurōbei.

Within minutes, The Wolf returned leading a middle-aged couple. Taking up the rear was The Crab. All four stopped in front of Tanaka.

The Wolf introduced the man and his wife, explaining that they managed an inn nearby.

After identifying himself, Tanaka asked the innkeeper, "So, you saw Shining Blade?"

"Yes, sir. It was him!"

Tanaka glanced at the wife. She responded with a vigorous nod.

"Why do you think it was Shining Blade?" Tanaka inquired.

The wife took a step forward, explaining, "Deputy inspector, we were on our way to the market, and one of our customers stopped us. He pointed down the street to a fellow coming our way and said, 'That's Shining Blade!'"

"What did the fellow look like?"

"He had two swords. Oh! And he was young and tall," answered the innkeeper.

"He had on a green jacket with a design of pine needles," the wife added. Pointing toward the left side of her own forehead, she stated, "Plus, he had a prominent scar on his temple."

"He walked right by us," the innkeeper declared. "We both saw him."

"When was this?" asked Tanaka.

"Yesterday, sir. Late in the afternoon."

"Where did the fellow go?"

"Into the market, sir. He went in the side entrance." The innkeeper looked at his wife and gestured for her to confirm his statement.

"That's right," the wife concurred. "And I think I saw him again later in the afternoon, sir. He was heading down an alley not far from here."

After posing several more questions, Tanaka thanked the man and his wife, telling them they were free to return to their inn.

Once the couple was gone, Tanaka gave his agents their orders. "Split up. The Wolf watches the side entrance of the market. The Crab goes to the front entrance. Find an inconspicuous spot. Observe who comes and goes. Wait and watch. I'll join you soon and stand somewhere you both can see me. Signal if you catch sight of the fugitive. I'll do the same. Understood?"

"Yes, sir," answered the two agents. Then they left to take up their posts.

After circling the market twice, Tanaka stopped in the shadowy entryway of a shuttered saké parlor, midway between his two agents.

What are the chances Kurōbei will come again today? the deputy inspector wondered, careful not to lean against the broken door behind him.

An hour or so later, Tanaka spotted a fellow striding down First Street, approaching from a distance. The fellow was too far away for Tanaka to see any scars on his face, but he was clearly young and tall with a pair of swords projecting from his sash, and he was wearing dark clothing.

Tanaka signaled his agents, alerting them to the possible presence of their man.

The fellow swaggered forward, looking perfectly at ease. Several blocks from the market's front entrance, he halted, taking up a spot at the side of the street. He scanned the block and, spreading his feet, crossed his arms over his chest as if waiting for someone.

Emerging from the shadows, Tanaka signaled his agents. The Wolf and The Crab moved inconspicuously to the deputy inspector's side. Tanaka turned his back on the fellow and ordered in a low voice, "Surround him and close in."

"Sir!" The Wolf exclaimed abruptly, gesturing with his chin toward the spot where the fellow had been standing.

Tanaka glanced over his shoulder and realized the fellow was gone.

"Follow me!" Tanaka ordered as he took the lead, hastening up the street. Within minutes, the three agents caught sight of their target, retreating rapidly eastward. The deputy inspector and his agents continued on, three blocks behind the figure. After several minutes, however, the fellow ducked into a small store selling housewares. Almost immediately, there was a loud crash, and merchandise began flying through the doorway, creating chaos outside on the street.

Tanaka and his agents rushed into the shop. They found the shop owner on the floor alone under a pile of baskets and brooms, blinking at them dumbfounded. As they helped him up, the proprietor told them what had just transpired.

The deputy inspector promised to return shortly, and they stepped back into the street.

Looking around, Tanaka growled in frustration, "Grr! That fellow created a commotion and slipped away."

The agents acknowledged their boss's frustration with frowns.

"Go question the locals again," Tanaka commanded. "I'll return to that housewares store to speak with the owner."

Leaving, the agents commenced their inquiries. Before long, The Crab brought a potential witness back to the store, where Tanaka was concluding his talk with the owner. The Crab introduced the witness, a young farmer who had seen something odd.

"I caught a glimpse east of here of a young man with a scar on his left temple," the witness told Tanaka. "I think it was Shining Blade. He was rushing up a northbound path toward Manshuin."

Tanaka and his agents took off up the main road, heading into the slopes. They searched the area where the farmer had seen the fugitive. After an hour combing the area and two additional hours expanding the perimeter of their hunt, Tanaka decided to call it quits. It had gotten dark, and no new witnesses had come forward.

"He slipped through our fingers *again*," Tanaka muttered as he led the two agents back to First Street Temple district, where he found a quiet teahouse. They entered, took seats and ordered food and drink. As they waited for the food to arrive, the agents quizzed Tanaka.

"Sir, do you think it's Ishida Kurōbei we're chasing?" queried The Crab.

"I do," Tanaka replied with a firm nod. "I'm convinced it's him."

"So, he's nearby," mumbled The Wolf. "At least there's some small satisfaction knowing we flushed him out at last."

"Right. This is the first time we've managed to send Kurōbei running," the deputy inspector remarked.

"We're making progress, sir," said The Crab, attempting to sound optimistic.

The Wolf scratched his chin and asked, "Sir, do you think it was Kurōbei who threw those scrolls during the Gion float procession?"

Nodding, Tanaka answered, "Kurōbei or his rōnin."

"And was Kurōbei behind the posting on those announcement boards outside Gion Shrine, sir?"

The deputy inspector responded by sucking air between his teeth, then stating, "I don't yet have proof, but he's my main suspect. Seems Kurōbei is stepping up his game—"

Tanaka stopped, seeing the waitress approach with a teapot and three cups. Once she'd dropped them off and had left, Tanaka reached out for the pot and filled the three cups. Each of the men picked up a cup, drank their tea and set their cup back down on the table.

"Sir, the message on those announcement boards—it was a public condemnation of the shōgun. Was it not, sir?" The Wolf asked with a frown.

"That's exactly what it was," Tanaka acknowledged. He sat still for a moment and then reached for the teapot and filled the cups again.

Tanaka continued, saying, "The magistrate is pleased that the two of you removed those announcement boards so quickly. I'm afraid, though, that word is spreading around town. Someone is threatening the Tokugawa. The magistrate is not happy about this situation."

"Sir, do you think Kurōbei's involved in planning a rōnin uprising?" asked The Crab.

"Apparently, he is."

"An uprising in Kyoto, sir?" The Crab inquired.

"Yes. A rōnin uprising in Kyoto with Kurōbei as the main organizer," the deputy inspector clarified.

The two agents shot worried glances at their boss.

"Things could get serious," Tanaka declared.

The Crab queried, "Sir, will Commissioner Wada be sending you directives tonight concerning our morning search?"

"No—" Tanaka hesitated. "Magistrate Gomi ordered *me* to oversee the arrest of Ishida Kurōbei."

"Commissioner Wada won't be involved?" asked The Crab.

"No." Tanaka squared his shoulders and explained, "The commissioner will be out of town for some time. The magistrate told me to take charge."

The Wolf and The Crab blinked hard, their expressions puzzled.

Then, lifting his chin, The Wolf declared, "You can count on me, deputy inspector."

"Me, too, sir. I'll be at your side," The Crab stated resolutely.

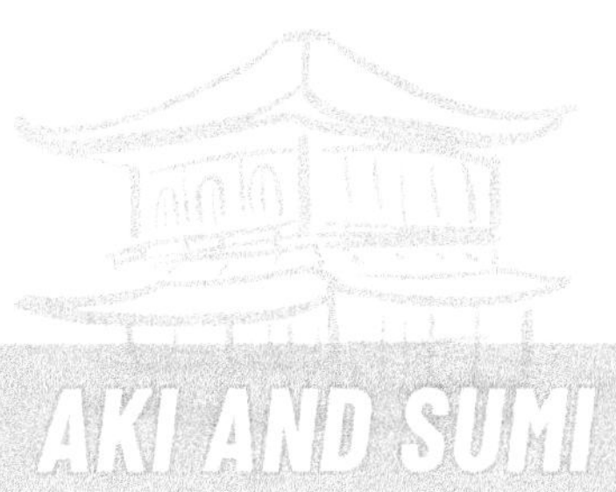

AKI AND SUMI

"Sister Aki!" called out the boney, young woman from the kitchen gate of the Konoe estate.

Aki had just turned down the alley, about to make her last delivery on another muggy morning. She looked up to see Sumi waiting for her, an anxious expression on her pock-marked face.

As she rushed toward Aki, Sumi blurted out, "I'm in love with Prince Toshitada!"

"You met Prince Toshitada?" asked Aki.

"Sort of. Well, let's say I saw him."

"Really?"

"Uh, huh! Prince Toshitada visited us a few days ago. He's so handsome. Like that prince from The Tale of Genji."

"The Tale of Genji?" Aki repeated, bending down to set her last bundle of kindling on the ground in the alley.

"Sister Aki! You've never heard of The Tale of Genji? He, he!" Sumi snickered.

Here she goes, Aki thought. She's already poking fun at me. "Sure, I have. I just didn't know—"

Sumi interrupted. "I love The Tale of Genji. So much flirtation and desire."

Aki pulled back her chin in dismay. "According to what I've heard, The Tale of Genji has a prestigious reputation. It's a classic from long ago."

"Sister Aki, you're not giving me a history lesson, are you? I only care about what's happening these days."

"You don't like history, Miss Sumi?"

"Definitely not. I'd love to meet Prince Genji, though." Sumi smiled, mischievously. "Too bad he's been dead for ten thousand years."

Aki shook her head.

"I think Prince Toshitada's as charming as Prince Genji!" Puckering up her lips, Sumi seemed to wrap her arms around someone taller than her before kissing the air.

Aggravated, Aki retorted, "The Tale of Genji isn't about sordid sensual pleasures." Hearing herself say those words, Aki felt odd. It hadn't sounded like something she'd say. She suspected she'd heard someone else use those very words, but she couldn't remember who exactly. Maybe Sister Bunkai.

"What do you mean, sordid?" Sumi's tone dripped with sarcasm. Then she lifted her nose in the air and made a funny face, saying, "Anyway, how would *you* know about sensual pleasures?"

"Ha!" Aki couldn't help laughing at the exaggerated tone of the maid's voice.

Sumi grabbed Aki's arm playfully, saying, "What do you think Prince Toshitada's Katsura estate is like?"

Determined to control herself, Aki answered in an even tone. "I don't know."

"He didn't whisper it in your ear?"

"He said—" Aki stopped. She caught herself just in time. She had vowed to keep her conversation with Prince Toshitada a secret. Until now, she had managed to stick to her promise, and she was determined to keep it that way. She responded, "Why would he talk to me?"

"Hmm!" Sumi arched her eyebrows and jumped to a new subject. "Prince Toshitada is generous, too. He sent the former head of the Konoe household a gift of rare Chinese incense made from camphor. It smelled awful—like pine sap or something—but the head of the household said camphor is good for treating ailments of the eyes, and he was suffering from blurry vision. That was for New Years a while back."

"You told me the former head of the household left the estate over a year ago, right?"

"No!" Sumi shot back. "He didn't leave. He *died*. And the new head is just a kid."

"Oh—"

Sumi interrupted. "The former head was like Prince Toshitada—always generous with gifts. Once he sent a splendid present to former reigning empress Meishō. It was a tray set on short legs, like a low table. On top were little shapes like lucky animals and plants, and it had all kinds of treats to eat."

"Oh! An island-stand!"

"Yeah. That's what they called it."

"Did they say the landscape was based on Mount Hōrai?"

Sumi frowned, wrinkling her nose and saying, "What?"

"Mount Hōrai. You know, Sister Sumi—the realm of the immortals."

"Achh!" Sumi moaned. "There you go again, lecturing me."

"No! I mean, I just thought you knew." Aki tried smoothing Sumi's ruffled feathers. "Those trays are used at picnics. I saw one being delivered to the Nijō residence not long ago."

"You did?" Sumi sounded peeved. "Anyway, the former empress sent the Konoe something nice in exchange."

"What did she send?"

"A koto. I suppose you know what that is, since you know everything."

"Oh, come on, Miss Sumi. I'm sorry I offended you."

"So, tell me. What's a koto?" Sumi demanded.

"It's a stringed instrument for playing music," Aki answered.

Sumi blinked and looked away, expressionless.

"Right?" asked Aki.

Sumi responded as if she'd totally forgotten everything they'd been discussing. "Sorry, what were you saying?"

"You're terrible, Miss Sumi!"

"Am I?" asked the maid, turning back to Aki with a quick smile. "Did I fool you just now, Miss Aki? I'm practicing how to mislead people. That way I can become a kunoichi."

"A what?"

"A kunoichi. You know, one of those female spies. They get to sneak around town and listen in on people at all times of day. That'd be fun, huh?"

"Well, I don't know. Sounds dangerous—"

Interrupting and looking suddenly worried, Sumi whispered, "Oh, I better get back. Let me go ahead of you, Sister Aki. Then after a few minutes, you follow me."

"Sure."

"Hope to see you again sometime. But if the master chef is around, I'll just stay mum. He'd probably accuse me of being lazy." With that, Sumi turned and scurried down the alley.

Aki waited until Sumi had passed through the side gate of the Konoe estate. Then, picking up her bundle of kindling, she followed the maid into the courtyard of the Konoe kitchen. Hearing a low voice, Aki glanced up to see the same bald man she had noticed in the shadowy entryway before. Aki guessed he was the master chef, the one Sumi had complained about.

Pointing to a spot near the doorway, the man said, "Set the kindling down there." Then he sank back into the interior.

After doing as she was directed, Aki went to a blue-lidded ceramic pot sitting nearby. She adjusted her wrist coverings, removed the lid and pulled out a letter. She slipped the letter up her sleeve, pressed it in next to two other letters and turned to walk away.

PART 5

IN 1654, A BIRD WINGING ITS WAY OVER WESTERN KYOTO couldn't help but notice a massive rectangular precinct surrounded by sloping stone ramparts and a double moat. Those below knew this as Second Street Castle, the shōgun's seat in Kyoto. A military stronghold and a staging ground for Tokugawa displays of power, Second Street Castle had been erected a half century earlier by the founding Tokugawa shōgun. Once finished, buttressing structures began rising up to the west, providing administrative headquarters for the governor, the magistrate and the commissioner. As you've no doubt grasped, Perceptive Reader, several of our main characters had offices in this district.

Closest to Second Street Castle was the headquarters of Itakura Shigemune, the Kyoto governor. Appointed by the shōgun, Governor Itakura had overseen Kyoto for over thirty years, just as his father had for nearly twenty years before him. The two Itakura governors had been responsible not only for shogunal administration and tax collection in Kyoto and its eight neighboring regions, but also for maintenance of Second Street Castle and supervision of the court, temples and shrines in the old capital.

Under the governor was the Second Street magistrate, Gomi Toyonao. A long-lived Tokugawa loyalist, Gomi was now in his twentieth year as Kyoto's chief of police and head jurist. Gomi's office was located west of the governor's headquarters on the grounds of Second Street Encampment, where he directed numerous bureaucrats and undercover agents.

Just as physical spaces proclaimed the privileged position of warrior officials, personal appearance revealed the men's high standing. Their formal wear included a starched vest with clan insignia and pleated, voluminous trousers worn over a fine robe. Everyday attire consisted of a wide-sleeved jacket and ankle-length, skirt-like trousers. Warriors carried two sheathed swords, one long and one short, inserted under a sash wrapped around the hips such that the hilts extended in front of the torso. The customary warrior hairstyle was a distinctive forward-swept topknot, waxed and set in place across a shaved pate.

A PRISON CELL FOR THE OUTLAW

"A PRISON AWAITS HIM," DECLARED TANAKA TAISUKE, DEPUTY inspector in the Office of the Kyoto Governor. He was referring to the rōnin outlaw Ishida Kurōbei.

"I see, sir," replied the undercover agent known as The Crab.

It was late on a hot afternoon, and the two men were leaning against a wall outside a fabric shop, keeping to the shade at one side of Imadegawa Street, north of the imperial palace. They were waiting for The Wolf to arrive.

"Sir, will you take Kurōbei to the tower prison at Second Street Castle?" asked The Crab. "I mean, once we catch him."

"That depends," Tanaka replied. "If we capture him in the next few days, we're to march him to the tower prison. After that, we're to take him to a new jail. It's a storehouse six blocks south of the tower prison. The commissioner's refurbishing it as a prison. When it's ready, that's where Kurōbei will sit."

"It was once a storehouse, sir?" asked The Crab, sounding uncertain.

"Yes. It's meant for a single, particularly troublesome prisoner who needs to be separated from others in the tower prison. Commissioner Wada said he'll provide stipulations for moving and guarding a prisoner there."

The Crab glanced to the left down Imadegawa Street and remarked under his breath, "Ah! Here he comes."

Looking over his shoulder, the deputy inspector saw The Wolf striding eastward toward them. Tanaka pushed himself off the wall and began walking at a brisk pace in the opposite direction. The Crab trailed behind him, and The Wolf remained farther back. The three men made their way to the Kamo River, crossed to the eastern side and then continued on to the First Street Temple district.

Several days earlier, after receiving reports of a suspicious stranger showing up near First Street Market, Tanaka and his agents began focusing on the northeastern neighborhood. They believed the stranger in question to be Kurōbei. Despite their best efforts, however, they'd failed to apprehend the rōnin. Then, that morning, an informant had come forward, claiming to have spotted a man matching Kurōbei's description entering a clothing shop near First Street Market. Tanaka had sent messages to The Wolf and The Crab, telling them to prepare for another evening hunt.

Before reaching the market, Tanaka stopped in a quiet, shaded spot under a willow tree, waited for the two agents to catch up and then issued his orders. They were to split up, one agent going north and the other south to question pedestrians and shopkeepers. The deputy inspector would enter the market to look around. They were to return to the spot under the willow within a half hour.

Tanaka headed off on his own into the market. After questioning several customers, he came upon one who claimed she'd seen a fellow resembling Kurōbei. The customer, a local woman buying carrots and burdock root, had spotted the fellow on her way to the market. He'd been rushing up a slope toward Shugakuin.

Wasting no time, Tanaka stepped out into the street, located The Wolf and The Crab and left the market behind. The three men hastened northward, up gravel lanes and narrow alleys. As they turned toward the east, their surroundings gradually changed. Closely packed residences and businesses gave way to a patchwork of small rice fields, clusters of fruit trees and thatched farmhouses.

Once they'd crossed the Otowa River and reached Shugakuin, Tanaka sent his agents to scout around. Meanwhile, he ducked behind a bamboo fence across from the front entrance to Enshōji and watched as the sun began casting long, purple shadows across the roadway.

After an hour, The Crab rejoined Tanaka behind the fence. The agent whispered, "Nothing to report, sir."

Tanaka nodded.

Using his chin to gesture across the roadway toward the Enshōji gate, The Crab whispered, "That convent's the residence of a former imperial princess. Is it not, sir?"

Tanaka nodded again and silently resumed his watch with twilight settling in. Some time later, he spotted The Wolf approaching.

The Wolf arrived with something significant to report. "Sir, I caught a glimpse of a figure. He was ducking through a grove of maple trees just north of Enshōji. I pursued him, but lost track of the fellow."

"Show us the spot," Tanaka ordered.

"Yes, sir." The Wolf started off again, leading Tanaka and The Crab into the lower, forested slopes of Mount Hiei. Above, clouds seemed frozen in place hiding the moon, while tiny flashes of pale illumination—fireflies flickering over the irrigation channels dug between terraced fields—punctuated the murky darkness.

The Wolf led the way past the side gate of Enshōji, before taking a narrow, uphill path to the north. He stopped and silently pointed toward a stand of maple trees. Tanaka gestured for The Wolf to move forward. The Wolf advanced slowly and entered the stand of maples. Tanaka and The Crab followed, careful to avoid stepping on a dry twig or slipping on a slimy rock. Even the slightest sound could alert the fugitive.

Encountering nothing suspicious, the three men climbed farther up the forested slope above Enshōji. When the trail petered out, they found themselves inching their way through thick undergrowth. Unable to see much of anything, they relied on their senses of touch and hearing. Tanaka had trained his agents for operations like this, but it ended up being a slog for all three of them.

Around midnight, Tanaka finally called off the search. Despite his determination to seize Kurōbei that evening and put an end to the rōnin's reign of lawlessness, Tanaka's efforts were in vain. Once again, the wily outlaw managed to slip through his grasp.

"AKI, COME HERE," NATSU ORDERED, CROSSING HER ARMS OVER her chest.

Aki was returning from her deliveries, about to open the gate to her yard. She stopped, seeing her mother standing near the doorway of their hut. Natsu wasn't alone. The village headman stood next to her. They both looked tense.

"Aki, the village headman needs to speak with you," Natsu stated.

The headman was a middle-aged fellow with a torso that looked as thick and solid as the trunk of one of the older trees on the mountainside. Having spent his life farming fields nearby, he had a tough streak and performed his duties with severe confidence.

"Yes, sir." Aki gave a small bow. "How may I be of service, sir?"

"Have you seen any suspicious individuals around here in the past few days?" the headman inquired, glowering at Aki.

"No. I haven't—" Aki stopped, cut off by her mother.

"Aki, the headman tells me an unfamiliar man was spotted near here. Have you noticed anyone?"

Aki shook her head.

Natsu faced the headman squarely, replying, "As you see, sir, my daughter hasn't run into any strangers, either. If we see an unfamiliar face, we'll let you know. Rest assured of that, sir." Natsu tucked her chin and placed her hands on her hips.

The headman grumbled. He stepped back, but, before leaving, he cautioned her, "You and your daughter must take care to avoid danger, Mistress Natsu."

Natsu dipped her head, acknowledging the headman's warning.

After bowing stiffly, the headman pivoted and marched away.

Once he was gone, Natsu headed straight to the hut and, opening the door, motioned for Aki to join her.

Inside, Aki sat at the edge of the raised plank flooring and removed her sandals. Then she turned and made her way to the sunken brazier, where she lowered herself onto one of the circular mats. Meanwhile, Natsu secured the door, crouched in front of the clay stove and prepared a fire. Once done, she removed her own sandals and joined her daughter.

"Mom, why did you secure the door? I still have to gather firewood."

Looking away, Natsu shrugged stiffly and replied, "I just wanted us to relax a bit before we start our chores."

"Mom, do you think it could've been Shining Blade spotted near here?"

Natsu shook her head apprehensively, answering, "Certainly not, Aki. Why would you ask that?"

"I heard he's been spotted in the Manshuin neighborhood."

"*That's* unlikely."

"Hmm," Aki mumbled, noticing how strangely her mother was acting. I know mom doesn't want me to worry, she said to herself. But our mountainside isn't as safe as I thought it was.

As Natsu reached up to untie the scarf wrapped around her hair, she remarked, "I noticed a lot of tangles under your scarf, Aki. This is a perfect time to work on each others' hair, don't you think?"

Aki nodded, saying, "You first." She stood to get the boxwood comb, and then, lowering herself to her knees behind her mother, she started combing Natsu's long, straight hair.

Clearing her throat, Natsu remarked teasingly, "Let me guess. I suppose you've got something to ask me. You've always got a question or two. What is it today?"

"Well—" Aki took a moment to think and started in, still running the comb through her mother's hair. "I heard there was a fire at the palace two years ago, and it was started by serving girls. Is that true?"

Natsu nodded. "Two serving girls set the fire. The girls admitted to it. They worked in lowly positions at the palace. Poor creatures—they're only twelve and thirteen years old."

"Really?"

"Yes. And, as it turns out, the same girls started other fires in town."

"They did!" Aki paused and, handing the comb to her mother, the women changed places.

Aki turned to a different subject as Natsu began removing tangles and smoothing down her daughter's wavy hair. "Sister Bunkai told me that the Sentō palace is where retired Emperor GoMizunoo resides."

"That's right."

"And next to it is the palace of his wife, former Empress Tōfukumon'in."

"Right," Natsu repeated, as she switched the comb from one hand to the other.

"She's the daughter of the second Tokugawa shōgun."

"Uh, huh. Sister Bunkai's been telling you a lot about the imperial family," Natsu observed.

"She had me copy an imperial genealogy," stated Aki.

Natsu had finally managed to get Aki's hair to behave and was now making long, even strokes with the comb. She grew quiet, concentrating on her work. It was Aki who broke the silence.

Sounding tentative, she asked, "Mom, did dad ever say anything to you about my birthmark?"

"He did." Natsu stopped the comb and added, "Your father told me he was concerned you'd become self conscious about that little mark when you grew up. He hoped you'd realize it doesn't mean anything."

Aki felt her cheeks burn as she stared down at the floor.

Natsu stood and returned the comb to a shelf nearby. She sighed deeply and stated, "We should start our chores."

COMMISSIONER WADA RETURNS

"Here to report to Commissioner Wada," Tanaka called out, standing at attention outside the large wooden gate of Second Street Encampment.

It was the first cool morning of the week, but Tanaka felt clammy and uncomfortable. He had shown up in response to a summons from his immediate superior, who had returned to town on the previous evening.

The two guards on duty, who were familiar with the deputy inspector, replied, "Yes, sir."

As one guard pulled on the heavy gate to open it from inside, the other emerged from his station and went to stand just inside the compound on the courtyard gravel. He was the senior guard, and he waited for the gate to open and Tanaka to step forward. Once Tanaka had entered the grounds, the senior guard turned to march across the courtyard, escorting the deputy inspector to Wada's office. The commissioner's office was located on the same compound as Magistrate Gomi's headquarters but in a separate building.

Tanaka remained four steps behind the guard as they moved forward. Although he knew the way, Tanaka needed to follow Wada's orders. He was to be escorted. Although unclear why the formality was necessary, the deputy inspector had little choice in the matter.

Outside Wada's office, the guard climbed a short flight of steps, turned onto a veranda and approached a closed door with the deputy inspector trailing behind him. Calling out, the guard announced their arrival. "Deputy Inspector Tanaka, here to see you, sir."

"Let him in," the commissioner replied, his response sounding more like a growl than spoken words.

When the guard slid the door open, Tanaka caught a glimpse inside of the small man he recognized as Wada. Wada sat across from him, hunched over a large desk covered with documents. Wada was unmistakable with his tall forehead, dark brows and hooded eyes. The commissioner quickly rolled up a scroll he'd been reading and, slouching to the side, he leaned on the armrest next to his desk. Without looking at Tanaka, he twisted his mouth to one side and gestured for the deputy inspector to enter and take a seat.

Tanaka squared his shoulders and crossed the threshold as directed. The guard remained on the veranda and slid the door closed before retreating.

Tanaka lowered himself onto a cushion, saying, "Welcome back, sir." Then he bowed deeply.

"Hm," Wada replied, barely acknowledging Tanaka's greeting.

The deputy inspector returned upright, focusing on the tatami in front of him.

Wada got down to business, stating, "Magistrate Gomi informed me that in my absence you oversaw the team searching for Shining Blade."

"That is correct, sir," Tanaka replied, knowing better than to tell his superior that it was the magistrate himself who'd ordered him to take charge of the Kurōbei case.

"What transpired?" Wada asked in his typically brusque manner.

"Sir, Ishida Kurōbei ruthlessly murdered four individuals. He trespassed on private property and committed all variety of other crimes from burglary to assault."

Wada interrupted, asking, "Kurōbei attacked the governor?"

Tanaka paused in surprise before quickly answering, "Yes, sir. At the Gion Festival, someone threw a scroll at Governor Itakura. The scroll contained a threat. We believe Kurōbei wrote it, sir."

"And?"

"I have organized a manhunt for the criminal, sir."

Wada sat up straight, pushing aside the armrest, "You've *not* found him!"

"No, sir." Tanaka extended his elbows out to the side and, pressing his palms flat on his thighs, he lowered his head and shoulders toward the tatami.

Wada jumped up from behind his desk and barked at Tanaka. "All this time, and you have not yet captured Kurōbei!"

"Unfortunately not, sir," Tanaka answered, bowing again.

"What've you been doing, Tanaka? Sitting on your haunches? Staring at the heavens?"

"No, sir. I have been directing agents across town. We have searched each district, twice. We now believe Kurōbei to be operating mostly in the northeastern part of town, sir."

Wada shouted, "Why aren't you there now, putting him in leg irons, Tanaka?"

"When you dismiss me, sir, I will depart directly for First Street Temple district!" Tanaka declared before dipping his head.

"Excuses! You give me excuses!" Now Wada picked up a book from his desk and threw it at Tanaka. The book slammed against one of Tanaka's shoulders and fell with a thud to the tatami.

Tanaka lowered his head in another deep bow, wondering what it would take to mollify Wada. When he sat back up, he realized that Wada was looming over him, face enraged, shoulders hunched forward and an arm overhead in the air. A snarl escaped from Wada's mouth as he swung the side of his raised hand at Tanaka. The deputy inspector felt a whack across his shoulders blades. Stunned, he tucked his chin and remained absolutely still.

Wada stomped back to his desk and dropped down on his cushion, cursing. After a moment, he added, "You are relieved of responsibility for overseeing the capture of Ishida Kurōbei."

"Yes, sir."

"You will no longer meet with Magistrate Gomi!" Wada exclaimed.

"Yes, sir."

"*I* will take charge of the Kurōbei investigation. You will receive written commands from me, and you will carry them out promptly. No more prevarication!"

"Understood, sir."

Glowering, Wada lifted his chin and peered down at Tanaka. Then he stated, "Prepare a detailed report of your activities and have it on my desk first thing tomorrow."

"Yes, sir."

Leaning back on his armrest, Wada spat out a final order. "Get to work, Tanaka."

"Yes, sir." Tanaka bowed deeply. Avoiding direct eye contact with Wada, he stood and left the commissioner's office, maintaining his formal bearing.

Tanaka closed the door, moved quickly down the veranda and crossed the courtyard, heading toward his residence.

I'm glad that's over! Tanaka thought with relief. It's not the first time Wada has chastised me, but it *is* the most unusual. Tanaka sucked in air between his teeth in disbelief. He couldn't help but wonder whether Wada had behaved so outrageously simply to stop him from asking questions—questions like, Where've you been? And what've you been doing?

✳ ✳ ✳

"Sir, here to report," The Wolf declared.

"Hm! Give me a minute. Take a seat," replied Tanaka, focusing on what he was writing at his desk. After finishing his last line, the deputy inspector set down his writing brush, glanced up at the agent and announced, "I've been relieved of command."

Taken aback, The Wolf asked, "Sir? What's that? You're no longer in charge of the Shining Blade case?"

"That's right. Commissioner Wada has taken that responsibility off my shoulders."

Frowning, The Wolf protested, "But, sir, Commissioner Wada doesn't know what's going on in town. He's been away. How does he think he can trap that snake Kurōbei? He'll be relying on the same team you had."

Remaining quiet, Tanaka shrugged his shoulders.

After waiting for a long moment, The Wolf asked, "Sir, do you know where Commissioner Wada's been lately?"

"I don't," Tanaka responded. He added in an uncharacteristically sarcastic tone, "Far be it for me to inquire."

"Of course, sir." The Wolf dropped his head.

Tanaka paused before adding, wryly, "If I'd tried to ask where he'd been, Wada would've flogged me with that writing brush of his."

The Wolf lifted his eyes to meet Tanaka's, the corners of his mouth turning up in a smile. Regaining his typically serious expression, the agent asked, "Has Commissioner Wada issued orders for us for this evening, sir?"

"I have yet to receive orders," Tanaka answered with a shake of his head.

"Should we conduct an in-town search as on previous nights, sir?"

Tanaka sat back, rubbing his forehead, and finally answered. "Yes, order evening patrols and stakeouts in town."

"Yes, sir," The Wolf replied before cocking his head and asking, "Sir, why did Wada reappear now?"

"I honestly don't know. He hasn't contacted me for weeks. And I haven't seen him among the officials gathered for recent events. I thought he'd vanished."

Reaching up and pushing a clump of hair off his forehead, The Wolf inquired, "Did Commissioner Wada tell you anything about his activities, sir?"

"No. Nothing. Wada gave me no explanation of what he's been doing."

"What about Magistrate Gomi, sir? Did he tell you anything?"

"No. And I will no longer be meeting with Magistrate Gomi, apparently."

"I see." The Wolf replied.

"THERE'S SOMETHING OVER THERE FOR YOU," BUNKAI remarked, pointing to a small item wrapped in silk sitting on Aki's desk.

Aki had just arrived at the Ryokuin'an study, finding her teacher at work. She glanced across the room and went to the smaller desk, where she lowered herself onto a cushion. Picking up the silk-wrapped item, she untied the knot and pulled back the fabric.

"A nuri uchiwa. I love it!" Aki exclaimed as she lifted the small fan by its lacquered bamboo handle. She studied the tiny gold squares affixed to one face. Carefully turning the fan over, she found painted on the reverse side a hill with a curving stream. The painter had used powdered malachite for the mossy green hill and pulverized lapis lazuli for the deep blue of the stream.

"This is what I see every day!" Aki enthused. "It's like the stream near my hut, the one running into the Otowa River. Thank you, Sister Bunkai."

"You're welcome, Aki. It's from all of us at the convent. It's to show our appreciation for you carrying the letters."

"I'm happy to help."

"And I'm glad to hear that," the nun replied. "You should know, Aki, before Prince Toshitada and his brother left the convent the other day, they told the reverend mother how pleased they are to have you carrying the secret letters."

"Really?" Pinching her eyebrows together in a frown, Aki was unable to fathom why delivering letters was so important.

"Yes," Bunkai answered before standing and moving toward Aki. She reached out, handing her student a scroll, rolled-up and secured with silk cord.

"That's today's lesson," the nun stated.

Aki nodded and unwound the cord to open the scroll. Smoothing the scroll out across her desk, she found scattered lines of writing covering the white paper surface. After identifying a few words in the first line, Aki glanced up and said questioningly, "What is this, Sister Bunkai?"

Still standing next to Aki, Bunkai explained, "It's a sequence of poems composed fifteen years ago at a party for Tanabata."

"The Star Festival? It's coming up soon, right?"

The nun nodded. "In two weeks."

"Would you read the first poem to me, Sister Bunkai?"

Peering over her student's shoulder, the nun read out in a clear voice, "The Star Festival. Let us celebrate the enduring prosperity that results from the emperor joining his heart with the hearts of his subjects, as they vow eternal devotion to one another, just like the festival stars."

"The festival stars—" Aki glanced up at her teacher. "They're husband and wife, right?"

"Yes," answered Bunkai as she moved back across the study to her own desk. "On the night they reunite, the Star Festival is held. You remember that from last year. Don't you, Aki?"

"Uh, huh. The two stars—the Weaver Maiden and her husband, the Cowherd—meet in the sky one night each summer."

"Precisely," Bunkai answered, lowering herself onto her cushion.

"I remember you telling me the nuns here gather to pray and offer fruit at the altar of the imperial family on that night."

"That's right. It's a simple ceremony at the convent. But the event is much more elaborate at court. Members of the imperial family write poems, listen to music and compete at the incense game."

"Speaking of the imperial family," Aki remarked casually, "would you tell me about the fire at the palace?"

"That's a leap!" Bunkai replied, but she proceeded to explain. "The fire occurred in early autumn. I heard that the flames spread rapidly due to the strong wind. Soon it was an inferno. Before firefighters could stop it, the flames consumed a number of buildings."

"Sister Bunkai, did it reach buildings where you used to work as a lady-in-waiting for the former empress?"

"It did. It destroyed the palace of the retired emperor and the adjoining palace where his consort lived. Flames leaped over the palace walls and even spread to buildings nearby. It was a horrible catastrophe. Taihen deshita."

Aki took a moment to consider the devastation before asking, "How did the fire start?"

Without answering, the nun took a deep breath and exhaled.

"Serving girls started it?" asked Aki.

Bunkai lowered her gaze. "I can't say for certain."

Aki peered at her teacher before moving on. "Sister Bunkai, I heard there was a thief spotted near here. He's called Shining Blade."

The nun lifted an eyebrow, looking up at Aki and saying, "Another bewildering leap!"

"Do you know anything about Shining Blade, Sister Bunkai?"

"I heard that a deputy inspector in the Kyoto Governor's Office is overseeing the case. He leads a team tracking that outlaw, so you don't need to worry about your safety here in the foothills, Aki."

Before she could pose her next question, Bunkai sat up straight and reached for a writing brush. "I have a document to complete, Aki. Focus on copying the Star Festival poems."

Aki prepared her ink and started her transcription. She filled a sheet of scrap paper with her writing, placed it on the tatami and started on a fresh sheet.

Several hours passed this way, until Aki heard Bunkai delicately clearing her throat. She looked up to see the nun putting away her writing utensils.

"It's time to conclude your lesson," Bunkai stated.

Aki straightened up her desk. Then, seeing the nun stand to leave, Aki did, as well. Aki picked up her gift, the oval fan, and waved it back and forth for her teacher to see. Smiling, she slipped the fan into the wide opening of her sleeve to carry it with her.

Bunkai went to the door and slid it open. But, after glancing into the courtyard, she turned back saying, "It's raining, Aki. Maybe you should stay a bit longer."

Happy to delay her departure, Aki retreated. Then, just as Bunkai was closing the door, a clap of thunder sounded in the distance.

"Looks like we'll have a little more time to talk, Aki."

Relieved to stay dry, Aki nodded and settled onto her cushion.

"What should we talk about?"

"The rōnin?" Aki suggested.

Bunkai tilted her head. "*You* will have to tell *me* about the rōnin, Aki. You know more than I do, I suspect."

"Well, would you just tell me your opinion, Sister Bunkai? Why do the rōnin oppose the Edo authorities?"

The nun paused. She seemed to be listening to the sound of rain dripping from the eaves. Finally, she responded, "From what I've heard, they believe Elders on the Edo Central Council are causing rōnin to suffer across the realm."

"And in your opinion, it that true?"

"Well—" Bunkai's voice trailed off.

Aki charged ahead, asking, "Why can't the rōnin simply become retainers of the Tokugawa shōgun? Wouldn't they be happy serving him or another Tokugawa lord?"

"The Tokugawa can't take on all those retainers. Their resources aren't limitless. And there are so many masterless warriors."

"I don't understand why those men don't find someone else to hire them."

"I'm sure they try. But it's not that easy. Many men have lost their position as retainers. There aren't enough jobs for all of them."

"There're that many rōnin?"

Bunkai nodded. "And given their plight, I suppose it's understandable that some rōnin end up resorting to extreme measures."

"Extreme measures? Like what?"

"Like seizing the emperor, for example."

"You mean, kidnapping the emperor?"

"Yes. Did you know, Aki, that leaders of the Edo Insurrection planned to kidnap his majesty? They were going to escort him out of the palace and take him someplace remote like Mount Yoshino."

"No!" Aki responded, incredulous. "They planned to force the emperor to leave the palace?"

"They said they would be *rescuing* the emperor."

"Why'd they want to do that?"

Bunkai shot her student a wary glance and replied, "To persuade him to support their cause."

Aki froze, not sure how to react.

"One thing is clear, the rōnin are victims of changing times. The world of sentient beings is filled with sorrow. That can't be denied." Bunkai stared resignedly across the room again.

Aki looked down at her lap, listening as the rain subsided and considering what Bunkai had just told her.

Finally, the nun spoke. "It sounds like the rain has stopped."

Aki lifted her head to listen. She mumbled, "Yes, it does."

"Let's see if the sun's coming out." Bunkai stood and went to open the door. Aki followed. Stepping onto the veranda, the two looked up into a clearing sky.

Noticing that the kitchen nuns were resuming their outdoor chores, Aki said, "I've taken so much of your time, Sister Bunkai. I should be going now."

"Alright, Aki. I'll see you tomorrow morning."

Aki thanked her teacher and left the study. Before long, she was heading home on a muddy path, her mind churning.

Are the Tokugawa just perpetuating rōnin suffering? Aki wondered. She recalled people saying that the Tokugawa shōgun had brought peace, delivering the realm from incessant wars. She'd presumed that people across the realm embraced Edo rule and happily obeyed the shōgun. Recently, though, she'd come to realize that wasn't true.

Maybe it's understandable that the rōnin in Edo revolted. If masterless warriors can't make a living, how can they care for their children and their aging parents? Maybe the only way for rōnin to make their case is by rebelling.

"DONE!" SAID AKI, FEELING PLEASED WITH HERSELF.

Having finished her morning deliveries in record time, she came to a stop in the middle of Third Street Bridge. Leaning over the railing, she gazed down at the Kamo River. Immediately below, a cluster of naked youngsters were hooting and cavorting in the water with their mothers watching from the bank. One young woman had stepped into the shallows to dip her baby, shrieking with delight, into the refreshing river. Farther off, a throng of older boys and girls were teasingly splashing and kicking water at one another. Suddenly, Aki stepped back and reached into her sleeve, worried that she'd misplaced the four letters she'd tucked away there. Finding the letters intact, she turned and set off eastward.

Aki decided to take a route different from her usual one. Within a half hour, she arrived at the lane leading to the Silver Pavilion. It felt like something was drawing her back. Glancing around, she spotted someone familiar.

There's Gohei! Aki realized.

Gohei, the gregarious middle-aged fellow, stood looking in Aki's direction. Noticing her, he began hobbling forward, leaning on a cane. An open, congenial expression animated the man's face. He yelled out a greeting. "Hello! What an unexpected surprise. Remember me? We met here recently."

Aki smiled. "I *do* remember you."

"I want to thank you for helping me the other day," Gohei stated. "My legs were giving me so much trouble. But they're better now. So, I wandered out for a stroll."

Aki wasn't sure what to say, but Gohei kept the conversation going. "Would you be so kind as to join me on the bench, young lady? I would certainly enjoy speaking with you again."

Aki responded hesitantly at first, but soon she was seated next to Gohei, listening to a lengthy disquisition on cuisine.

"I'm trying to decide where to go for dinner tonight," Gohei remarked, smacking his lips. Lifting a bushy eyebrow and shotting Aki a quick glance, he asked, "Ever tasted carp boiled in thick red miso?"

Aki shook her head.

"That's a no? How about grilled trout that was caught that very morning in the Kamo River?"

"I don't think so," Aki responded, looking uncertain.

"No? I've got to tell you, young miss—it's very tasty. Not to be missed. How about bass from the Yodo River? Or shrimp so fresh they jump off your plate? Odori ebi!" Gohei lifted his arms and wiggled them about.

Aki continued shaking her head. She sensed Gohei was trying to make her laugh, but she felt too uncertain to relax. She wondered whether she should be sitting there with him.

He went on. "That reminds me, do you like entertainments?"

"Um, sure. I do."

"I just love the acrobats at the dry riverbed, young miss. And the dancers performing on the stages at Fourth Street. I was planning to go down there to watch them, but their show's been cancelled. Ever since the government outlawed young men's kabuki, there's been trouble. They better watch out! Those people along the Kamo River have got to be careful. When the police show up, the entertainers scatter like dried leaves in an autumn wind." Gohei swung his head dispiritedly. Then he went on without missing a beat. "As far as I'm concerned, no disruption occurs when hardworking citizens take off a few minutes to enjoy a lively show. How can it hurt anyone to watch a man spinning a dish on a stick!"

Aki blinked hard.

"Right? Does my opinion make sense?"

Gohei's comments seemed perfectly reasonable to Aki. But before she could respond, Gohei had started up again, now expounding on the differences between Kyoto and Edo. When he finally came to a stop, he eyed her and asked casually, "Say, I hate being rude, but I never learned your name, young lady. Would you be so kind as to tell me?"

"I'm Yamanaka Aki."

"Lovely name. Do you prefer being called Miss Yamanaka or Miss Aki?"

"Miss Aki. Ha, ha!" She chuckled awkwardly, staring at her sandals. No one had asked her that question before.

He's interesting, thought Aki. But I'm not sure I should be sitting at the side of the road talking to a stranger.

"As I was about to say," Gohei continued. "Big things are always happening in Edo. It sure was crazy up there three years ago. Say, young lady, ever heard of the Edo rōnin uprising?"

"You mean the Edo Insurrection of 1651?" Aki asked. Then, leaning toward Gohei and seeing him nod, Aki spoke up, glad she had something to add. "Yes, I have heard of it. Rōnin plotted to attack Edo Castle. My teacher, Sister Bunkai, told me about it."

"Did she?" Gohei glanced at Aki, seemingly impressed.

"Yes. She said those rōnin were very unhappy. They'd lost their positions and got expelled from their domains. They had nowhere to go. Shōsetsu helped them. He encouraged them to improve their sword-fighting skills." Aki stopped abruptly.

Gohei nodded. "It's true, young lady. In fact, Shōsetsu opened a school for displaced men. They could meet other rōnin there and commiserate. People need to find solace somewhere. It's as natural as the sun rising in the east."

Leaning forward with interest, Aki was now gazing directly at the man. She caught herself and sat back, looking straight ahead.

"Young lady, has anyone ever told you the number of men willing to call Shōsetsu commander?"

Aki shook her head.

"Four thousand. Can you believe it? And those men weren't a bunch of low ranking misfits. Shōsetsu had influential associates and friends in high places. One man in his circle was the son of the first Tokugawa shōgun."

"The first shōgun's son?" Aki asked, eyes widening.

"Uh, huh. In the end, the Tokugawa protected him. He never faced the cruel tortures that others did."

"Really," Aki murmured.

Just then, a young couple came walking toward the bench where Aki and Gohei were sitting. Examining a printed map, they stopped nearby. They looked like tourists and were discussing the Silver Pavilion.

Gohei became quiet, tapping his foot. Aki sensed Gohei was anxious for the couple to leave, not wanting them hearing what he had to say.

Finally, Gohei turned to Aki and announced, "I think it's time for me to be moving along, Miss Aki."

"Oh! Goodbye, Mister Gohei." That was all Aki had time to say before her new acquaintance had stood, and—taking his cane in his right hand and using it to steady himself—he began hobbling up the road toward the Silver Pavilion. Within a minute, the young couple had left as well, going in the same direction as Gohei.

Aki sat still for a while, thinking. Mister Gohei is a great source of information, she said to herself. But I wish he could have stayed longer. I wonder what he thinks about the rōnin in Kyoto, like Shining Blade.

I need to get some answers, Aki decided. Maybe from Granny Mari—she knows what's going on, and I've got to pick up provisions for the convent. Without wasting another moment, Aki rose to her feet and set off for Yamabana Market.

*　　*　　*

"Hi, Granny Mari," Aki called out, heading across the crowded market.

Just finishing a sale, the wizened stall keeper was handing a bunch of turnip greens to a local housewife with a curt, "Off you go!"

Aki stopped abruptly and, as she waited for the housewife to leave, she ran the back of her hand across her sweaty forehead.

Mari turned to Aki with a greeting. "Hello, young miss!"

Stepping forward, Aki remarked, "Another scorcher out there!"

"Yup. When will we get some relief?"

Anxiously to learn something new, Aki jumped to her first question. "Say, have you heard anything about troubles facing the rōnin, Granny Mari?"

"The rōnin?" Mari replied, wiping her hands on her apron. "I know lots of people who feel sorry for those warriors who've lost their masters. Especially the rōnin who can't make it on their own."

"Why can't they?"

"Too many rules and regulations," Mari replied.

"Like what rules and regulations?"

"The ones coming from Edo. It's all over my head, though."

"Oh! How about the first shōgun's son? Did you hear he supported Yui Shōsetsu?"

"Yui Shōsetsu?" Mari asked, now looking cross. Aki couldn't tell if the stall keeper was aggravated because she didn't know or because she wasn't comfortable talking about it.

With a little shake of her head, Aki paused and changed the subject. "How about Shining Blade? Heard anything new about him?"

"The rōnin thief?" Leaning over her counter, Mari whispered, "He was spotted up your way, Little Aki."

Aki recalled the village headman's warning, but she decided to play dumb, saying, "In Shugakuin?"

"Yup," answered Mari before pressing her lips together. She eyed Aki warily and added, "Mistress Natsu can tell you more about it."

"*You* don't know anything else?" Aki asked.

"Nope," Mari replied, before reaching under her counter and pulling out a bundle of provisions wrapped in a large fabric square. Moving the bundle across the countertop, Mari mumbled, "Ask your mother."

Aki decided not to push the stall keeper any farther. With a nod, she took the package from Mari's leathery hands, pivoted and set off for Enshōji.

Strange, Aki thought as she walked away. Mari has always been happy to share what she's heard. She's usually the biggest gossip in the market, but today she's holding back. Why does she think my mom will tell me anything more about Shining Blade? My mom is becoming more close-mouthed every day.

Upon arriving at Enshōji, Aki headed to the kitchen to drop off the provisions. She found the kitchen nuns cleaning pots with no time to talk, so she left for home.

*   *   *

Arriving home late in the afternoon, Aki found the yard empty. The hut was empty, as well, and her mother was nowhere nearby. After finishing her chores and preparing dinner, Aki retreated indoors and took a seat at the short table, where she waited. An hour passed, and Aki started getting hungry, so she ate by herself, taking her time as she chewed on a few final grains of rice and millet, savoring their mildly sweet flavor.

It was twilight when Natsu finally returned. She looked tired and irritable, and she smelled sweaty. Natsu cleaned up in the yard and came to sit with Aki at the table. Picking up her bowl and a pair of chopsticks, she began scooping food into her mouth.

"Want some cucumber?" Aki offered, pushing a small ceramic bowl across the table toward her mother.

Natsu reached into the bowl with her chopsticks and took several thin, green-rimmed disks, tasted them and muttered, "Too tart."

Feeling a bit stung, Aki replied, "Sorry."

"You ate already?" Natsu inquired.

"Uh, huh." Aki answered, wondering why her mother seemed out of sorts.

After taking another bite of cucumber, Natsu remarked, "Too much vinegar."

"Sorry," Aki repeated.

Natsu pushed aside the cucumbers and finished her millet and rice. Other than the sound of Natsu's chopsticks scraping against the sides of her bowl, the hut was quiet.

When she was finished, she turned to her daughter, asking, "Anything happen today?"

"Not really." Aki shrugged and began to say, "Mom, can I ask you—"

Interrupting in an exasperated tone, Natsu remarked, "Can't it wait until tomorrow, Aki? I'm just so tired. All I want to do is eat and lie down."

Aki responded with a frown, "Alright."

Mom really *is* in a bad mood, Aki realized. I better forget about my questions. Maybe she'll feel better tomorrow. I'll ask her in the morning about Shining Blade and the son of the first shōgun.

PART 6

DETERMINED READER, BY NOW YOU REALIZE THAT AUTHORI-ties were struggling in 1654 to maintain law and order in the old capital. Like many other cities, Kyoto was teeming with resentful rōnin bent on challenging Tokugawa authority. From his office on Second Street Encampment, Magistrate Gomi oversaw the many guards, jailors, advisors, clerks and spies who assisted the Tokugawa in uncovering and quelling rōnin disturbances.

The undercover agents—both shinobi, or male spies, and their female counterparts, kunoichi—had been trained as experts at subterfuge, conducting surveillance and gathering intelligence. They had learned how to dress in disguise, one day as an itinerant laborer and the next day as a doctor, a farmer or a peddler. Whether scouring city streets for criminals or traveling busy highways to track the spread of gossip, their service was essential to the Tokugawa.

Undercover agents in Kyoto faced a special challenge since the old capital was the home of a powerful symbolic figure—the emperor. Occupying the place of honor at the heart of the old capital, the emperor was considered a descendent of the sun goddess, who could ensure the prosperity of his subjects through his wisdom and justice. Accordingly, if an emperor rose up against a shogunal regime, he might just topple that military government. Thus, as you can imagine, Dear Reader, a key concern for shogunal authorities in Kyoto was the possibility of a rōnin leader gaining the emperor's support, whether by gentle persuasion or by aggressive action such as kidnapping the monarch.

"Here! You'll need one of these to wrap around your head," explained Deputy Inspector Tanaka as he handed a long strip of white fabric to each of the two young women at his side.

"Yes, sir," replied the women, called The Stork and The Mouse. They were kunoichi who'd recently joined the ranks of undercover agents employed by the Office of the Kyoto Governor.

It was early morning, and the deputy inspector had summoned the two kunoichi to the warehouse storing agents' disguises. Not far from Second Street Encampment, the warehouse was filled with garments and accessories. It had caps stacked on shelves, robes hanging from hooks, wigs perched on stands and footwear scattered across the floor. Tanaka stood near the middle of the warehouse, advising the kunoichi on how to dress like female peddlers from Katsura. He had assigned them to day patrol in the busy downtown area. Tanaka had chosen it as a safe place for the two newly-minted kunoichi to launch their undercover work, since Shining Blade hadn't been spotted downtown for some time.

"You'll want to wear leggings and heavily-used robes like these," Tanaka added, pointing to the indigo-dyed garments folded and crammed into a huge chest.

"Yes, sir," said each of the kunoichi before grabbing a robe and leggings and piling them atop the armful of garments she'd already taken.

The Mouse, who had a small mole on her left cheek, asked in a soft voice, "Deputy inspector, should we wash these garments before returning them?"

Tanaka dipped his head, answering, "I appreciate your concern, but that won't be necessary. I'll likely need you in the field again tomorrow. Hold on to the garments to wear them then."

"Yes, sir," replied The Mouse.

After pointing out a place in the back room where the kunoichi could change, Tanaka wandered off to a far side of the warehouse, looking for a pair of peddlers' backpacks. Before long, he returned holding two packs with dangling straps. That was just as the women emerged from the back room wearing dark blue leggings, a robe of woven hemp and a strip of white fabric wrapped around their heads with the ends tied in a small bow at the forehead. The outfit served as the traditional attire for female peddlers who brought sweet fish from the Katsura River and vegetables from nearby farms to sell in town.

Setting down the two backpacks, Tanaka began instructing the women on their patrol. "After you leave here, head east, stop at the market to buy fish and greens for your baskets. Then make your way to the Kamo

River and stop at the spot we agreed on for you to sell your fish."

"Yes, sir," answered the kunoichi in unison, while strapping on their backpacks.

"Be careful today. Don't wander off. Don't follow anyone," Tanaka warned.

"We'll be careful, sir," replied The Mouse.

"Stay at your post and observe," stated Tanaka, continuing with his instructions. "If you see someone who matches Ishida Kurōbei's description, leave your post together—not alone—and go directly to inform The Wolf. He'll be standing on the east side of Third Street Bridge."

The deputy inspector checked the women's packs while reviewing secret signals for their patrol. Just as the deputy inspector was about to send the two kunoichi off, the door of the warehouse opened, and The Wolf and The Crab stepped in.

Lowering their heads toward their boss and the kunoichi, the two agents called out, "Good morning."

Tanaka answered the approaching agents resolutely, saying, "It'll be a good morning if we arrest Kurōbei."

"We'll do our utmost, sir," The Wolf replied with a determined nod.

Turning back to the kunoichi, Tanaka ordered the women to report to him at his residence by sundown. The two agreed and set off from the warehouse.

With that, the deputy inspector glanced at The Wolf and The Crab, stating, "Time for us to decide on disguises for ourselves."

* * *

Walking at a leisurely pace, Tanaka made his way down a sunny Third Street, heading toward the Kamo River. He was outfitted in gardening gear—fabric arm cuffs, a mud-spattered jacket and a headscarf to hide his shaved pate. Trailing a half block behind him was The Crab.

The deputy inspector slowed, hearing several loud voices and spotting three men outside a paper supply shop. Deciding to listen in, Tanaka stopped nearby in a patch of shade. The shop proprietor was complaining about taxes and seeking agreement from two customers.

Tanaka scratched his chin. Then, glancing around, he noticed a figure in the distance rushing toward him on Third Street. It was The Wolf, dressed as a carpenter in a heavy, pocketed apron. Tanaka stepped away from the beleaguered proprietor and took up a quieter spot where he could hear what The Wolf had to report. The Crab joined him.

"Sir!" exclaimed The Wolf as he came to an abrupt stop next to his boss, panting and wiping sweat from his brow.

"Yes?" whispered Tanaka.

The Wolf reached into a pocket and pulled out a piece of cloth. Extending his hand toward the deputy inspector, the agent opened his fist and said, "Sir!"

Tanaka looked down at the cloth dangling from the agent's hand, realizing that the white strip of fabric was stained with blood. Tanaka tensed his jaw, grabbed the strip and replied, "This isn't good."

His voice low, The Wolf pointed to the fabric and added, "A boy ran by with that in his hands."

"Where were you?" Tanaka asked, as he refolded the strip to conceal the bright red splotches.

"Standing on the east side of Third Street Bridge, sir. The kid said he was going to the police box. I took it from him and explained I'd deliver it to the police. The kid told me he'd seen a tough guy—a fellow with two swords and a scar on his left temple—who grabbed a Katsura peddler. He held a dagger to her neck and dragged her down an alley. That's when her scarf fell off."

"Did the boy show you which alley?" the deputy inspector asked, tucking the blood-splattered fabric up his sleeve.

"He did."

"Take me there," Tanaka demanded.

"Yes, sir." The Wolf turned and took off, running to the alley with Tanaka and The Crab close behind.

Arriving in no time, Tanaka paused and directed The Wolf and The Crab to stay close. Peering down the narrow alley and seeing nothing suspicious, Tanaka pulled out his dagger. He cautiously entered the alley with the two agents directly behind him. After stopping and waiting for his eyes to adjust to the dim surroundings, the deputy inspector bent his knees slightly and crept forward. He could see now that the alley was a block long with several doorways, all of which were closed except one standing partly open all the way at the end. Tanaka snuck up to a stack of wooden boxes and craned his neck to check behind them. The Wolf and The Crab followed, each grasping a dagger. Finding nothing, they advanced deeper into the shadows and soon reached the end of the alley. Tanaka turned back to the two agents and silently indicated with a hand gesture that they needed to check to see what was behind the partially open door.

Tanaka stepped forward and pushed the door open. Sticking his head inside, he realized that the doorway led to a storeroom at the back of a shop selling ceramic kitchen wares. The deputy inspector scanned rows of shelves stacked with pots, jugs, plates and bowls. His eyes landed on a group of shelves to his left that were empty and tilted sideways. Below those shelves, piles of smashed ceramics littered the dirt floor. Clearly, a struggle had taken place here.

Tanaka's eyes scanned to the right. Suddenly, he pulled his chin back and froze. The Wolf approached and, after looking over Tanaka's shoulder, he took an abrupt step back into the alley and stopped. The Crab came and, catching a glimpse, gasped.

In a pool of light from the open door, a woman lay stretched out and unmoving on the floor with her face turned away. She was dressed in an indigo-dyed jacket and leggings, both stained darkly with her blood. Tanaka and the agents recognized her instantly. It was The Mouse, one of the kunoichi they'd sent off from the warehouse that morning, dressed as a Katsura peddler. The Mouse was dead, her arms stretched out as if reaching for the door.

Tanaka stepped over the threshold into the storeroom, crouched down and gently turned the kunoichi's head, finding it still warm. Eyes open, she stared off in a permanent state of shock. The kunoichi's pale neck was marked by a small wound, but her torso—from her left shoulder down to her abdomen—bore a deep gash where the blade of a sword had sliced into her body, killing her.

Shocked, Tanaka's face went slack. Still crouching, he lost his balance and toppled back, now sitting in the dirt.

"Sir!" The Wolf exclaimed, bending down behind Tanaka and clasping the deputy inspector's shoulders for support. "Are you alright, sir?"

"Give me a moment," Tanaka mumbled. He took a deep breath and slowly let it out as The Wolf stepped away. Peering into the dark corners of the storeroom, the deputy inspector rose up, whispering to his agents, "The assailant may still be here. Look around."

The Wolf and The Crab each gave a quick nod and turned to search the storeroom. They moved forward in the dark and carefully skirted around shelves stacked with ceramics. Less than a minute passed before The Crab called out, "Over here!"

Tanaka and The Wolf hurried to join The Crab, looking down at a male figure sprawled out on his belly in the shadows, not far from The Mouse's corpse. His head was partly covered by his torn jacket, and a long sword lay at his side. Its steel blade was covered with blood. Shards of a large pot were scattered around the man's body.

The Crab looked up at the deputy inspector, saying, "Sir, it looks like he was knocked unconscious by a pot smashed over his head."

"Turn him over so we can see his face. Beware!" ordered Tanaka.

Bending down, The Crab did as he was told, revealing the man's face. A jagged scar marked his left temple. The

Crab shot his boss a quick glance, exclaiming, "Sir, it's Shining Blade!"

Tanaka stepped forward to get a better look and then turned to The Wolf, telling him to bind the man's wrists behind his back.

The Wolf pulled a length of rope from a pocket in his apron and knelt down opposite The Crab to secure the unconscious man's hands. Then the two agents returned upright.

"Is it Kurōbei, sir?" asked The Wolf.

"I believe so," answered the deputy inspector before turning to The Crab and saying, "Go to the nearest police box. Bring officers with two stretchers and blankets."

"Yes, sir," The Crab responded, dipping his head and rushing off.

"You stay here," Tanaka ordered The Wolf. "Don't let him out of your sight. I'll go and deal with the gawkers."

"Yes, sir."

Tanaka staggered toward the storeroom door, passing the dead kunoichi. As he caught of glimpse of her pale face, the deputy inspector felt a great weight pressing down on him. He continued on into the alley and halted at the entrance, where he squinted in the bright sunlight. Finding himself wobbly, Tanaka breathed deeply, spread his feet and set his fists on his hips. Standing like that, the deputy inspector looked strong and stable. In truth, he felt he could be knocked down by a feather.

"Good morning, sir," said The Wolf, ready to report.

The agent had returned to the deputy inspector's study on the morning after the arrest of the outlaw rōnin, Ishida Kurōbei.

"Hm," replied Tanaka without setting down his writing brush or looking up from his desk.

Neither Tanaka nor The Wolf had slept much the night before. They'd been sitting in the study for a long while consoling The Stork, the female agent who'd just lost her partner. The young kunoichi was finding it hard to accept that at one moment her fellow agent, The Mouse, had been standing beside her saying she needed to find a toilet and, just a short while later, The Mouse was found dead, murdered by Ishida Kurōbei.

Tanaka had learned a few things from The Stork concerning events of the previous day and had developed a general idea what had transpired. He had refrained from probing too deeply, though. He could do that another time. After the grieving kunoichi had finally left in a state of exhausted distress, leaning on The Wolf's shoulder, Tanaka had finished a report addressed to Commissioner Wada. Then he had delivered the report personally, returned home to eat dinner and retired to his bed. He had tried to sleep, but in vain. Now, the deputy inspector was writing a letter.

Waiting for Tanaka to finish, The Wolf sat looking around the study. It was the middle of the morning, but outside the skies had darkened under a heavy cloud cover, and inside it looked as if night had fallen. Two candles burned on tall iron stands beside Tanaka's desk. Their flames cast flickering shadows that danced jerkily across the long wall behind the deputy inspector. The Wolf blinked several times as he tried to clear his burning eyes. Then he frowned, hearing the pattering of rain on the roof.

"There, that's done," Tanaka mumbled miserably, shaking his head and setting down his brush. He added, "I'll need you to get this letter to a courier. It should be posted this afternoon."

"Yes, sir," The Wolf replied with a nod.

"But give it a few minutes. It's raining. Let's sit and talk. With any luck, it'll clear up soon." Tanaka began folding the letter he'd just finished, explaining, "This is a note expressing my regrets and informing The Mouse's family that she died in the line of duty."

Responding softly and sadly, The Wolf said, "I see, sir."

Tanaka set the folded letter down on the desktop in front of him and stared at it.

The study became quiet as the two men sat listening to the rain. Then a crack of thunder jolted them from their gloomy thoughts.

Tanaka glanced up and, with a dark shadow falling across his face, he said in a bitter tone, "I failed to protect her from Kurōbei. I should've known she wasn't ready for the field."

The Wolf responded sympathetically, asking, "How could you have known, sir?"

Tanaka shook his head, remaining silent.

Changing the subject, The Wolf inquired, "Have you heard anything about Kurōbei's condition this morning, sir?"

"Wada contacted me a short while ago to inform me Kurōbei still hasn't regained consciousness. He's to remain in the emergency clinic at Second Street Castle until he does."

"I see," The Wolf replied.

"The worst thing is, Wada didn't even ask about that poor kunoichi. She offered up her life for this Office, and he didn't even mention her name."

The Wolf let out a ragged sigh. "One of his own gets killed—a vulnerable young agent—and he just brushes it off, sir?"

Tanaka shook his head in frustration, his brow furrowed.

The Wolf changed the subject again, now remarking, "The Mouse must've torn away from Kurōbei's grasp and clubbed him over the head. She landed a serious blow! Don't you think, sir?"

"Yes. She apparently used one of the biggest pots in that storeroom. But at the very moment her pot hit Kurōbei's head, his blade was slicing through her torso. If only she'd have escaped." Tanaka dropped his glance. Then, quickly looking up again with a low snarl, he said, "I could've strangled Kurōbei when we found him in that storeroom stretched out in the dirt."

"As could I have, sir.

Tanaka shook his head, slowly letting out a breath. Then, fixing his eyes on the folded letter in front on him, he said, "I can't get that poor woman's face out of my mind."

"You're not alone, sir."

After a long pause, The Wolf changed the subject, asking, "What do you think of Kurōbei stealing that box of letters from the Nijō estate, sir? I can understand why he stole swords from the downtown shop and money from the Katō residence, but I still don't understand why Kurōbei wanted those letters."

"Right—" Tanaka's voice faded as he looked over The Wolf's shoulder, across the room.

"Sir, do you have any idea what was in the letters?"

Tanaka answered slowly. "It dawns on me that those letters provided information about the emperor's schedule. Lord Nijō is the imperial regent, after all."

"Ah! How could I have overlooked that fact! Does that mean—"

"It means Kurōbei wanted to find out the emperor's schedule," Tanaka answered. "Perhaps he wanted to identify the best time to abduct his majesty."

The Wolf pulled his chin back and, looking through his bushy eyebrows at his boss, he asked, "Do you think Kurōbei was about to kidnap the emperor, sir?"

After rubbing his forehead for a moment, Tanaka replied, "It's possible."

"Then it's a good thing that scoundrel is behind bars, sir!"

"Indeed."

"Sir, maybe we can sleep for the first time in weeks, knowing that Kurōbei won't be causing any more trouble."

"Yes, let's get some sleep tonight."

"Sir—" The Wolf hesitated before going on. "Why do you think Kurōbei has been so bent on causing terror? I mean, I understand that he's a rōnin, and rōnin face serious difficulties. But not all rōnin go around killing innocent people left and right."

Nodding, Tanaka replied, "Perhaps he's simply obsessed. On the other hand, there's much we don't know. Circumstances certainly encouraged him to act."

The Wolf paused in thought for a long moment before continuing. "Sir, I don't want to overstep my position, but can I ask, is Commissioner Wada up to something?"

Tanaka tilted his head, peering at The Wolf, and answered, "Such as?"

"The way Wada comes and goes—is it just me, sir? Or do you find it odd, too?"

Tanaka let out a quick snort, replying, "No, it's not just you. *I* certainly can't figure it out. But there's something we have to consider—Wada may have received orders from Governor Itakura to travel the realm on secret business, and Wada may have been told not to share the details with me. For all I know, the governor ordered Wada not to speak about the matter with anyone."

"Understood, sir." The Wolf paused before asking, "You don't think Wada's tangled up in something underhanded. Do you, sir?"

"I don't know," Tanaka responded, leaning forward. "But it's clear to me we shouldn't dig too deep. If Wada's been involved in suspicious activities, we need to turn a blind eye."

"Understood, sir." The Wolf repeated. As he nodded, a shaggy clump of hair fell across his eyes.

"In fact, based on what I've seen, I suspect we'll never find out what Wada's been involved in," Tanaka stated. "It'll be swept up and hidden away."

Pushing the hair from his eyes, The Wolf declared knowingly, "Those at the top see no reason to share what's really going on with those of us below."

"Exactly," replied Tanaka.

"I've got so many questions. Every time I answer one, three more pop up," Aki complained.

"Aki, I know how that feels," the nun Bunkai replied. "It happens to me, as well."

"Does it? It seems like nothing bothers you. You're so peaceful, Sister Bunkai."

"I try to be. But it's hard work."

Aki was sitting at her desk in the Ryokuin'an study, taking a break from her morning lesson. Across from her sat Bunkai at her own desk.

Bunkai added, "It's understandable you have questions, Aki. Your upbringing was rather sheltered."

Aki cocked her head, saying, "You think so?"

"Yes. You're an only child. I'm sure Mistress Natsu has been careful to protect you."

"Uh, huh. I guess I'm all she's got."

"No doubt she's concerned for your safety. It must be hard for you, though. A person with a curious mind like you will find it hard to set aside your questions."

Aki sighed. "Is it even possible for a person to set aside their questions?"

"It is," Bunkai smiled. "I recommend you try."

"But didn't you tell me my curiosity is a blessing, Sister Bunkai?"

The nun looked her student in the eye and answered, "I did. However, that doesn't mean you should let your curiosity get the upper hand. You have to learn to tame your mind, Aki."

Aki nodded and grew quiet. At last, she added, "Sister Bunkai, I appreciate how patient you've been with me."

"That's my job as your teacher," Bunkai answered. She added, "There's no rush, Aki. Over time, things will become clearer. Feel free to ask me any questions that come to mind."

Aki nodded and picked up her writing brush. Instead of resuming her copying, though, she set her brush back down and reached into her sleeve. Gently removing the small oval fan her teacher had given her recently, she said, "Sister Bunkai—"

The nun glanced up from her desk and, seeing the fan, stated, "You've got the nuriuchiwa with you today!"

"Uh, huh. Thank you again, Sister Bunkai. It's so pretty."

"I'm glad you like it, Aki. You earned it," responded the nun. "You've helped us enormously by carrying those letters for the reverend mother."

Aki dipped her head and looked back down, resuming her work. Some time later, when Aki heard papers rustling from Bunkai's direction, she glanced up to see her teacher straightening papers and preparing to leave the study. Aki began clearing her desk, as well, realizing her lesson was coming to an end. Once she had returned her writing utensils to their lacquered box and had neatly stacked her sheets of practice paper atop the desktop, Aki looked over at her teacher again.

Bunkai, who had been waiting for Aki to finish, remarked, "Little by little, you're seeing things as they are."

Aki nodded, not sure what Bunkai meant, but understanding that her teacher intended it as a compliment.

"Remember, Aki, effort will never betray you," Bunkai added. "I'll see you tomorrow morning."

"Uh, huh. I'll be here first thing. Thank you, Sister Bunkai."

"Of course. Be careful, Aki."

"I will."

Within minutes, Aki was passing through the side gate of the convent and heading down the narrow walkway toward the main Shugakuin road. The area was bathed in the warmth of the midday sun, and for Aki it felt good to be out, after sitting inside all morning.

Aki ambled along, listening to the buzzing of insects. Despite the heat, she decided to take the long way home, strolling along the Otowa River. When she reached a shady spot under a stand of cherry trees, she left the roadway and stood at the river's edge. She remained there for some time looking down into the rushing current, mesmerized by the movement of the rapids and feeling the gentle spray of water on her cheeks. Finally turning around, Aki stepped back into the bright sunlight on the roadway and headed toward the pine-covered slope.

Aki passed by farms and fields, noticing that locals had started binding bunches of herbs at the stem and hanging them upside down from the eaves of their barns. In the fields, tall green stalks of grain were bending in the wind, moving up and down like waves on an ocean. A gentle breeze carried moisture from the fields and sent a subtle, sweet aroma Aki's way. It smelled like the breath of a sleeping baby. With a light step, Aki entered the cool of the forested foothills, returning home.

EPILOGUE

Tenacious Reader, persistence pays off. You've followed Deputy Inspector Tanaka and his undercover agents as they searched in and around Kyoto, pursuing the slippery villain Ishida Kurōbei. In your dedication to reaching a conclusion, you've ensured that Tanaka and his agents capture Kurōbei, ending his threat of a rōnin insurrection in Kyoto. Now that Kurōbei has been detained, Aki and her mother can breathe a sigh of relief, feeling safe once again on the streets of the old capital and the narrow trails of the forested slopes.

No doubt, questions remain. They will be answered in due time, however. Consider this, Dear Reader, further adventures await!

GLOSSARY

Abunai desu yo!: It's dangerous!

Atsui: hot.

Bodhisattva (bosatsu): one on the path to Buddhahood or a savior being worshipped by Buddhists.

Brother of the sun goddess (Izanagi no Mikoto): the creator god in the Shinto pantheon.

Buddhist chanting and prayers (shōmyō): conducted at temples and convents in the morning, midday, afternoon and evening; including sutra recitation.

Buddhist precepts: a central aspect of Zen practice; principles adopted in ordination.

Burdock root (gobō): a starchy root vegetable shaped like a carrot, enjoyed for its crunchiness and sweet taste.

Buta ni shinju: pearls for a pig.

Chimaki: glutinous rice wrapped in bamboo leaves.

Code of the samurai (bushi no reigi sahō): traditional etiquette for and expectations of a warrior; codified in a variety of different school formulas.

Cut the straw rope (shimenawakiri): to initiate a festival by cutting a straw rope draped around or across sacred objects and locations.

Dance of the hernshaws (Sagi mai): dance performed by two men dressed like a male and a female bird near the float of European magpies at the Gion Festival.

Dō shita no?: What happened?

Dorobō: thief.

Edo Insurrection of 1651: an unsuccessful plot to attack Edo Castle planned by a group of rōnin intending to bring down the Tokugawa regime; led by the martial instructor Yui Shōsetsu (1605–51), who owned a shop selling armor, and Marubashi Chūya (?–1651), a trained staff fighter; also known as the Keian Uprising, the Tosa Conspiracy and other names.

Effort will never betray you (Doryoku wa uragiranai): hard work leads to success.

Emperor GoKōmyō (1633–54; reigned 1643–54): son of retired Emperor GoMizunoo and half-brother of the Enshōji abbess.

Emperor GoMizunoo (1596–1680): now the retired emperor (reigned 1611–29); father of current Emperor GoKōmyō and the Enshōji abbess. The second Tokugawa shōgun arranged for the marriage of his daughter, Masako, to Emperor GoMizunoo; the wedding took place in 1620; after GoMizunoo's retirement, this woman was known as Tōfukumon'in (1607–78).

Empress Meishō (1623–96; reigned 1630–43): former reigning empress; Abbess Bunchi's younger half sister; the daughter of Emperor GoMizunoo and Empress Tōfukumon'in.

Enshōji: an imperial convent of Rinzai Zen Buddhism; located at Shugakuin in northeastern Kyoto.

First Street Temple (Ichijōji) district: an eastern Kyoto district located between the Takano River and the eastern foothills; considered a separate village.

Folding fan (hiogi): a collapsible, hand-held fan; often made from thick paper evenly folded and glued to cypress blades.

Fourth and Karasuma: an intersection of two streets near the center of downtown Kyoto.

Fourth shōgun = Tokugawa Ietsuna (1641–80; ruled 1651–80): great grandson of the founding Tokugawa shōgun; succeeded his father at the age of eleven; until 1663, Ietsuna's advisors were responsible for most governmental decisions; this was the first occasion in which power was held by the Edo Elders, a group of advisors, instead of a Tokugawa shōgun.

Fukuchiyama domain leader = Inaba Norimichi (1603–48): warrior and head of a domain in Tanba not far from Kyoto; he committed ritual suicide after being accused a leading a rebellion against the shogunate.

Geta clogs: elevated sandal-like footwear made traditionally from wood with a fabric or leather thong running between the big toe and the second toe; often with tall pegs or teeth below.

Gion deities: Gozu Tennō, his wife and their eight children.

Gion Festival (Gion matsuri): held in the seventh month in downtown Kyoto since 869; including two parades of floats to appease spirits blamed for plagues.

Gion Festival float procession = in this era, there were two Gion Festival float processions: an opening procession on the seventh day of the sixth month of the lunar calendar and a closing procession on the fourteenth day of the sixth month; on the seventh day, the floats left from the intersection of Fourth Street and Karasuma Avenue and moved east on Fourth Street, turned toward the south at Teramachi Avenue, then went west on Matsubara Street; leaving early in the morning, they paraded throughout the morning. The largest of the Gion floats were so heavy and unwieldly, unable to turn at intersections, that the combined exertion of many men became a spectacle attracting the crowd's interest at the festival called, Turning the wheeled floats (tsujimawashi).

Gion Festival floats: the Shinto floats (hoko) included the Benkei on the Bridge float (Hashibenkeiyama) dedicated to a hero of ancient times named Benkei; the Halberd float (Naginataboko), which had attached to its central pole a finial shaped like a halberd (a long pole-like weapon with a blade at one end); the Mountain-grotto float (Iwatoyama) also called the Stone-door float; and the Renunciate's float (Hōkaboko), the tallest of the Gion Festival floats.

Gion Festival music (Kyoto gion-bayashi): music of the Gion Festival played mostly by men on traditional Japanese instruments, meant to placate the gods.

Go: a Chinese board game in which two players compete, trying to surround territory with markers.

God of the grotto (Tajikarao no mikoto): god of " heaven-hand power"; a male god with tremendous strength.

Hachijō: an aristocratic family with a residence near the Kyoto imperial palace. First head of the family was Hachijō Toshihito (1579–1629), an imperial prince and the younger brother of Emperor GoYōzei. He was adopted by Toyotomi Hideyoshi in 1589, after Hideyoshi's son had died, leaving him without an heir. The emperor agreed and gave Hideyoshi permission to adopt his own younger brother, Prince Toshihito. Later, when his wife had a son, Hideyoshi disinherited Toshihito, but provided him funds to build Katsura Villa. The second head of the family was Hachijō Toshitada (1619–62), first cousin once removed of retired Emperor GoMizunoo.

Hai!: Yes!

Handscroll: a horizontal scroll in various lengths, usually with a surface of paper or silk; a main format for texts and paintings in premodern Japan.

Hidoi!: It's terrible!

Hōkyōji: a convent overseen by woman from the imperial family; located north and west of the imperial palace in Kyoto.

Hungry ghosts (gaki; Sanskrit:preta): unhappy spirits that, according to Buddhist lore, face hunger and thirst.

Ichijō: an aristocratic family with a residence near the Kyoto imperial palace. Ichijō Akiyoshi (1605–72), also known as Kanetō, was the tonsured brother of retired Emperor GoMizunoo.

Ii tenki desu ne?: It's nice weather, isn't it?

Inari shrine (Inari jinja): a Shinto shrine dedicated to the fox god, associated with prosperity.

Jissōin: a convent in Kyoto overseen by woman from the imperial family.

Kabuki: traditional popular form of theater with boldly stylized singing and dancing.

Kamo River (Kamogawa): a river that flows from the northeast into Kyoto and joins with the Takano River.

Kanpai: Cheers.

Katsura Villa: a residence-and-garden estate developed by Prince Hachijō Toshihito (1579–1629) and extended upon by his son, Prince Toshitada.

Konoe: an aristocratic family with a residence near the Kyoto imperial palace; the former head of the family was Konoe Hisatsugu (1622–53); the new head of the family was Konoe Motohiro (1648–1722).

Koro, koro: onomatopoeia for the sound of crickets.

Koto: a long, stringed musical instrument.

Kyoto governor: highest official in Kyoto serving the Edo shogunal government; responsible for shogunal administration and tax collection, oversight of the court, temples and shrines and maintenance of Second Street Castle.

Marubashi Chūya (?–1651): martial arts instructor; a trained spear fighter; he was crucified after it was discovered he had helped to organize the Edo Insurrection of 1651.

Minamiza Theater: the main kabuki theater in Kyoto, located on Fourth Street near the Kamo River.

Mount Hōrai (Chinese: Penglai): an imaginary island, home of immortals in the East China Sea.

Mount Yoshino: mountain located in Nara Prefecture south of Kyoto; in the fourteenth century, Emperor GoDaigo established here a breakaway Southern Court.

Mushiatsui: Hot and humid weather.

Nagataniden: a residence located in Iwakura, north of Kyoto.

Nijō: an aristocratic family with a residence near the Kyoto imperial palace; the current head was Nijō Mitsuhira (1624–82), a court nobleman who married Princess Yoshiko (1632–96), daughter of GoMizunoo and Tōfukumon'in.

Nuri uchiwa: a hand-held oval fan with a fixed handle made often of bamboo.

Odori ebi: "dancing shrimp"; raw shrimp.

Office of the Kyoto Governor (Kyōto shoshidai): bureau of the Edo government in the old capital; overseen by a governor, appointed by the shōgun and Elders of the Central Council in Edo.

Otowa River (Otowagawa): a river running from the foothills of Mount Hiei, joining with the Takano River.

Ox-headed heavenly king (Gozu Tennō; Sanskrit: Gavagriva): originally an Indian deity considered the king of the devas and a protector against illness.

Palace fire: in the summer of 1652, the Kyoto imperial precinct suffered extensive damage from a fire; later, several serving girls were found guilty of setting the fire.

Palanquin (norimono): a covered litter; a vehicle without wheels that holds one person; the box-like litter is suspended from a single long pole, which was thick and sturdy and which was carried on the shoulders of two, four, or six porters.

Peko, peko!: onomatopeia for a growling stomach.

Pickled white radish (daikon misozuke): slices of large radish preserved in fermented soybean paste, or miso.

Prince Genji: a fictional character; a handsome, artistically gifted courtier, also known as the Shining Prince.

Ryokuin'an: subtemple of Enshōji; residence of the nun Katatsuki Shōshin and her daughter, Kūgon Bunkai.

Sacred child (chigo): a boy wearing makeup and a ceremonial robe for the Gion Festival; chosen from among merchant houses in Kyoto as the sacred page of the Gion deities.

Sacred palanquins (mikoshi): temporary shrines for transporting Shinto gods.

Second Street Castle (Nijōjō): Kyoto headquarters of the Tokugawa shōguns; built in western Kyoto in the early seventeenth century by Tokugawa Ieyasu, it had become a staging ground for Tokugawa ceremonies and events.

Second Street Encampment (Nijō jinya): a precinct west of the estate of the Kyoto governor; location of the magistrate's office.

Second Street magistrate (Daikan bugyō): Gomi Toyonao; leader of the civil and judicial administration of Kyoto and its eight neighboring regions; serving the Edo shogunal government.

Shell matching game (kai-awase): game in which players attempt to match scenes painted on the inner surface of a set of clamshells.

Shi (し): a character in Japanese hiragana script meaning death, among other things.

Shigata ga arimasen: There's nothing I/we can do about it.

Shiin: onomatopoeia for the sound of silence.

Shōgōin: a temple in Kyoto overseen by a man from the imperial family.

Shoji doors (shōji): sliding doors with a lattice framework covered with thick paper, which is often white and semi-transparent; the doors slide in tracks set into the structure above and below the doors.

Shugakuin (Shūgakuin): a district of Kyoto, northeast of downtown, in the foothills of Mount Hiei.

Silver Pavilion: a building at Jishōji, a Zen temple in eastern Kyoto, also called the Temple of the Silver Pavilion (Ginkakuji); a two-storied structure in the retirement villa built for a shōgun in the fifteenth century.

Sun goddess (Amaterasu Ōmikami): chief deity in the Shinto pantheon.

Sutra: Buddhist scripture; some with passages considered as the recorded teachings of the Buddha.

Tabi socks: split-toe socks that reach to the ankle, easily worn with geta clogs.

Taihen deshita: It was terrible.

Taikō = Toyotomi Hideyoshi (1536–98): Japan's leading military lord in the late sixteenth century; the second of three great unifiers of early modern Japan; he advanced rapidly through echelons at court to the high post of chief regent to the emperor; after stepping down, he was called the retired imperial regent or Taikō. The Taikō gave Prince Toshihito land at Katsura on the southwestern outskirts of Kyoto; Toshihito developed a villa-and-garden estate there.

Takano River (Takanogawa): a river that flows through the northern part of Kyoto and joins with the Kamo River.

Tale of Genji (Genji monogatari): a lengthy novel; the leading character is a courtier named Genji; acclaimed as a classic of court literature, it is attributed to Murasaki Shikibu (ca. 978–ca. 1016).

Tanabata: the Star Festival; a traditional Japanese festival of mid summer, originating from an ancient Chinese legend; held on the seventh day of the seventh month of the lunar calendar.

Tanba: a province of old Japan close to Kyoto.

Tatami mats: rectangular flooring mats of standard size, about .9 meters by 1.8 meters, covered with woven soft rush straw and edged in fabric; commonly filled with rice straw.

Teinei na kotoba: formal way of speaking.

Temporary resting place (yorishiro): an object in which a Shinto god can take up residence during ceremonies.

Third shōgun = Tokugawa Iemitsu (1604–51; ruled 1623–51): grandson of the founding Tokugawa shōgun.

Tōfukumon'in (1607–78): the former empress; the daughter of the second Tokugawa shōgun, known early in life as Tokugawa Masako; her marriage to Emperor GoMizunoo was arranged to unite the shogunal and imperial families.

Uniform (hitatare): a standard warrior costume with two elements, a long-sleeved jacket and wide, skirt-like trousers (hakama). For formal occasions, warrior elite donned a two-part outfit (kamishimo), consisting of a sleeveless jacket and wide, pleated trousers worn over a robe.

Veranda: in traditional Japanese architecture, a roofed hallway, open at one side and raised off the ground, running along the perimeter of sections of a building; usually with polished wooden floorboards; from the veranda, sliding doors provide entry into the interior. The veranda often forms a zigzag, bending at 45 degree angles and creating a staggered profile, which, when the sliding doors are open, allows for optimal views of the garden from the interior.

Warrior's hairstyle: a shaved pate with long hair at the sides pulled back and up into a topknot called sakayaki.

Wide-mouthed jar (kame): ceramic vessel used for storing foodstuffs.

Wind chimes (fūrin): traditional chimes take the shape of inverted teacups made from various materials including iron, glass and stoneware; the chime has a long slip of dyed paper hanging from a clapper inside the cup; when the wind catches the slip of paper, the clapper swings and strikes the inner surface of the cup and makes a pleasant tinkling or ringing.

Wooden practice blades (bokken): weapons used by warriors for training and sparing; shaped basically like a steel blade but less expensive and safer to use than a real sword; coming a variety of lengths; used in kenjutsu, aikidō, kendō and other martial arts.

Yasaka pagoda: a five-storied structure near Gion Shrine, 46 meters in height.

Yōkai: supernatural creatures such as animal spirits, demons and monsters of Japanese folklore.

Yui Shōsetsu (1605–51): a rōnin and martial arts instructor; owner of a shop selling armor; a leader of the Edo Insurrection of 1651 meant to bring down the Tokugawa regime.

Zannen!: Too bad!